D1606781

Roads to Hilton Head Island

ROADS TO HILTON HEAD ISLAND

A Novel by David Baehren

iUniverse, Inc.
New York Lincoln Shanghai

Roads to Hilton Head Island

Copyright © 2005 by David F Baehren

All rights reserved. No part of this book may be used or reproduced by any means, graphic, electronic, or mechanical, including photocopying, recording, taping or by any information storage retrieval system without the written permission of the publisher except in the case of brief quotations embodied in critical articles and reviews.

iUniverse books may be ordered through booksellers or by contacting:

iUniverse
2021 Pine Lake Road, Suite 100
Lincoln, NE 68512
www.iuniverse.com
1-800-Authors (1-800-288-4677)

This is a work of fiction. Names of characters and businesses and events depicted are fictional or used fictitiously. Any resemblance to organizations or to persons living or dead is coincidental.

ISBN: 0-595-34836-X (pbk)
ISBN: 0-595-67160-8 (cloth)

Printed in the United States of America

DEDICATION

For my wife, Sonja. I love you.

Author's Note

Even though this is a work of fiction, I have tried to make descriptions of Hilton Head as accurate as possible. Some things are made up in order to make the story work. These characters are windows, not mirrors. No one should hold them up to look for themselves. While one might draw several parallels, I am not Peter Fredericks and references to his fictional family should not raise questions about my family. I had a very happy childhood and I am having a happy adulthood as well.

A few years ago, on a ride home from Hilton Head, my wife suggested that I should write this story. By the end of our long ride, the core of this story crystallized. I enjoy a full work and volunteer schedule, so this has been a long but fulfilling process. There were many starts and stops for various reasons. I have many to thank for their help along the way. Most importantly I thank my wife, Sonja, and children Ben and Sarah, for their patience, love, and understanding. My sister, Christine Barabasz, provided encouragement and edited early manuscripts. Steve Baehren, brother and Marine veteran of two wars, gave me insight for the prologue. Maria Siegel and Sonja Scott read early versions of this work. They won't recognize much in the final version. I spent a very interesting afternoon with LTJG Greg Houghton and LTJG Thomas Bolin of the United States Coast Guard, Air Station Detroit. Thanks for their help and for their service to our country. Ellen Critchley (CritchleyCreative.com) helped with preparation of the final manuscript and cover design. Special thanks go to my editor, Diane O'Connell (wordsintoprint.org), for her wisdom, guidance, and perseverance. Finally, thanks to Steve Caywood and Dr. Fred Higgins.

PROLOGUE

▼

January 1967, Da Nang, South Vietnam

The squad of twelve had been on patrol since midnight from an outpost near the South Boung River four miles east of Da Nang. This was a live fire zone, but they had seen no Viet Cong that night. Only explosions from occasional rocket fire rumbled in the distance. They set the wire on the far side of the paddy. Any VC that tripped the wire got it from land mines. Those who didn't get tagged got to bask in the illumination of trip flares. Then the hand grenades would rain down death.

"Sun's comin' up soon, lieutenant," Private Buddy Duke whispered as he crouched six feet into the jungle from the edge of a rice paddy.

"If you say so. This fog's so damn thick, I can't see the end of my pecker," Lieutenant Bennett replied without a smile. "Listen, when we're alone, you can still call me Mort."

"Thanks. Anything to make home a little closer helps. Man, I been dreamin' of crabs and corn on the cob and a cold one."

"Yeah, you're buyin' when we get back to Beaufort," Bennett said as he nudged him with his elbow.

All were tired and cold from a night in the jungle, especially Buddy Duke who was new to the Marines and even newer to Vietnam. The cold, the bad food, the nighttime maneuvers, and the constant danger made his adjustment to life as a rifleman in a combat zone difficult. Three weeks before, he had lived in the relative comfort of a transport ship on the South China Sea. A year before that he played football at Beaufort High School and made passes at cheerleaders.

"You and I are movin' out to the edge of this rice paddy," Bennett said without emotion. "We'll pick up Sanders and Sergeant Coswell down the way. Wanna put a couple of Claymores at the edge of a dike 'bout a hundred meters south. VC been crossing on that dike after sunrise."

The two stepped softly to reach Coswell and Sanders forty meters to the south. Memories of home came to Buddy as he labored to lift his soggy boots with each step. Three years before, Dick Coswell, Mort Bennett, and Buddy's older brother Leland allowed Buddy to tag along one Friday night. They drank whiskey on the beach of Fripp Island until they were nearly blind. Leland drove their father's sedan into the marsh on St. Helena on the way home. After a tow truck pulled them out, they spent the next hour pulling spartina grass out of the wheel wells.

His heart pounded and sweat beaded on his forehead as they sneaked along the edge of the rice paddy. His own body odor grossed him out. It was then that Buddy first truly regretted his decision to enlist four months out of high school. Buddy was happy that Mort Bennett had taken him under his wing, but if he had his choice, he'd be back in the Low Country doing just about anything else but sneaking around in the fog and placing land mines. Dick Coswell and Scotty Sanders were ready to go when Buddy and Mort arrived.

"Sanders, you lead," Bennett said. "Safeties off. If it moves, kill it."

"Yes, lieutenant," the two privates said in unison.

Happy to be off the lead, Buddy got in step six feet behind Sanders. In spite of the cool temperature, sweat soaked his underwear. His hands trembled. Ready to climb out of his skin, every step Buddy took required effort and concentration.

"Stop about 20 meters up," Bennett said in a forced whisper.

Like a wet blanket, fog still hung over them. The rising sun made it easier to see but this was no consolation for Buddy. The VC could see him just as well. He hated being exposed as they walked. At least sitting back in the jungle, he could sit protected by the dense foliage. Through the fog, Buddy spied a shape moving quickly across the next dike over. Before Bennett or Coswell could warn him, Buddy was down on a knee and fired two rounds. High-pitched wailing lasted about twenty seconds, then quiet. Buddy knew he had done something wrong before he took his rifle off his shoulder.

"What the hell was that?" Buddy said after the other three dropped to their knees to join him.

"You zipped a damn rock ape, Buddy," Coswell said. "Don't worry about it. Just don't shoot anything that's less than four feet. Got it?"

"Yes, sir."

"Anyway, use your grenades. Then they can't tell where it came from."

This completely freaked out Buddy. He'd never killed anything but fish. Buddy didn't even hunt ducks. He wasn't sure how he would feel when he got around to killing VC, but he didn't like how it felt to kill an unarmed ape.

"Sanders, radio back to let the others know to sit tight. Let's move."

Still shaking, Buddy lost his balance getting up. He fell forward with his M16 pointing at Sanders. The weapon fired and Sanders dropped backwards into the water. Coswell and Bennett looked at each other knowingly.

"Oh, shit. Oh, shit. Man, what did I do?" Buddy yelled as he got up to check on Sanders. He threw his arms in the air and motioned at Sanders. "Come on man, get up. We gotta get the hell outa here."

"Shut up and get back down," Coswell barked. "Come on. Let's pull him out."

Buddy crawled on all fours to Sanders. He rocked back and forth, crying hysterically. "Goddamn, I didn't mean it. Sanders, come on. Get up man."

"Buddy," Bennett hissed slowly and deliberately, "shut the hell up, or *I'm* gonna shoot you."

Buddy shut up, but continued to rock back and forth and sniffle. Coswell and Bennett pulled Sanders from the water, flipped off his helmet and checked for a pulse.

"He's dead, Buddy," Bennett said with resignation.

The three stared at the body. Brain tissue and blood streamed across his face. The skull above Sander's left eye was blasted open. Buddy sat back, put his hands over his face and cried in silence. He could barely fathom what he had done. Bennett and Coswell crouched by the body to give Buddy time to collect himself.

Bennett patted Buddy on the back and then reached into the side of Buddy's pack and pulled out a grenade. He pulled the pin and hurled it to the other dike. The explosion caused water to spout and rain down on the dead ape.

"Mort, what are you doing?" Coswell said as he crouched by Sanders.

"Sanders got it from the VC. Are you with me on this?"

"Don't know, man. We could get fried for this," Coswell said as he put Sanders' rifle on safety.

"This can go two ways, Dick. One: Sanders' parents learn their kid got it from an accidental discharge and died for nothin' plus Buddy's ass is in a sling. Two: Sanders' parents have some small amount of goddamn consolation from this bullshit and Buddy's butt is out of the sling."

"OK, Mort," Coswell said. "You radio the squad. You'll do a better job makin' it sound right. Buddy, not a damn word about this to anybody. Man, do you owe us."

Paralyzed, Buddy sat shaking with his arms around his knees. He had no idea how he would live with this—assuming he even lived through his tour.

"Get your shit together, Buddy," Mort said without consolation. "If this is gonna work, you gotta put on *the show*."

CHAPTER 1

▼

As she had been doing once a month for the previous four years, Patty Corry, Ph.D., waited patiently outside the office of her most important and most difficult patient. Young, energetic, and well-dressed staff members scurried in and out with no clue of her purpose while Patty reviewed notes from the last session. For all they knew she was a lobbyist, a White House aide, or a rich constituent. She looked like someone with money. With her brunette hair trimmed at her shoulders in a striking page-boy cut, perfect nails, subtle yet expensive accessories, smart-looking Liz Claiborne eyewear, and a sleek black wool suit, Patty had the entire package together. And she did have money. All but one of her patients paid $150 per hour up front for the privilege of seeing her at her office in Rockville, Maryland. She charged an extra $100 per hour to come to the Russell Senate Office Building.

A serious middle-aged secretary approached Patty, who was lost in thought. "The senator will see you now, Miss West."

Patty recommended using the false name. She, better than anyone in the Washington area, knew the stigma that came with seeing a psychologist. Triple that if you were an elected official. The secretary showed Patty in and closed the door as she backed out.

Buddy motioned for Patty to sit in one of two wing chairs in the corner of the office. Buddy poured two glasses of water and sat in the opposite wing chair. He loosened his tie and took a swallow of water. This helped him to switch gears. *Man not senator. Catcher not pitcher. Thinker not aggressor.* Nobody but his wife got to see this side of Buddy and nobody but Patty talked to Buddy the way she did. She was also only one of three people in the world who knew Buddy shot Scotty Sanders dead in a rice paddy in Vietnam.

"Take a few deep breaths, Buddy. Exhale fully. I need you with me completely. Feel the cares of the minute leave us. Go to a peaceful dimension."

Patty knew Buddy didn't have time to waste. His unique position made finding time for sessions difficult so she needed to make the most of every session. Buddy was a tough nut to crack. CEOs, lawyers, doctors, and politicians always were. This type of patient saw his illness as something outside of himself that he could think through. They were too smart for their own good. Alcohol, drugs, and marital affairs were common ailments that complicated post traumatic stress disorder. Buddy was no exception. They had made progress for the first three years of treatment, but Patty felt they were in a rut. She had a plan to change that.

"Before we start talking, I have a suggestion for you," Patty said as she crossed her long slender legs. Buddy knew not to even think about those legs. "I know you're not interested in group therapy for obvious reasons and traditional group therapy wouldn't help you anyway. This is something different."

Patty had been working with an emergency physician who suffered from post traumatic stress. He too had fallen into a rut and was making little progress. She felt that bringing the two together in therapy might get them both back on course.

"I think you would like Peter. He is your intellectual peer and he knows how to keep a secret. He does it every day at the hospital."

"I don't know," Buddy said, leaning forward with an elbow on his knee. I don't like the idea of somebody else being in on this little secret I got."

"Think of it this way. You know I think you should wait another four years to run for the nomination. I think you're not ready for that burden. I also know you're going to do it anyway. You need to start making progress again if you want to survive the campaign. This is the best advice I have for you. Think of me as another political adviser if you have to."

"Man, you shoulda been a labor negotiator," Buddy said with a smile.

"Life's a negotiation," Patty said with a broad smile. "You know that better than I do. What do you say?"

"All right. But we still gotta meet here."

"Deal. I'll make the arrangements."

"So, who is this guy?"

CHAPTER 2

▼

(Six months later)

"Dr. Fredericks, EMS is five minutes out with a six-month male who is choking."

It had been a lazy afternoon in the ER at Parkside Hospital when Peter Fredericks lay down for a catnap—a rare opportunity to grab some much-needed sleep. The nurse's voice over the intercom caused him to sit up and put his size 11 feet on the floor, a habit he developed in residency to avoid falling back asleep after being awakened.

"How old?"

"Six months."

"Coming. Call respiratory stat and get out the pediatric crash cart."

He did his best to fix the bed head in his thick curly brown hair and hastily tucked his loosely fit green scrub top in around his thin waist. His heartbeat accelerated as he walked to the treatment area of the emergency department of Parkview Hospital in Rockville, Maryland. Much of the hospital had been updated over the years, but the ER had been ignored and outgrown for years. Pete felt that the dingy floors, off-green walls, stained curtains that separated the small treatment rooms, and a hodgepodge of hand-me-down medical equipment all gave the feel of a third world clinic. He knew all the excuses from administration by heart. Tight budget. Cost overruns in the cardiology unit. Plan to build a new ER—no sense fixing up the place now. *That'll be the day. These walls will be green when I'm balding.*

Pete felt comfortable caring for children, but he knew a choking infant makes every doctor uptight. Airway problems were tough enough in adults. But in infants, they could be a nightmare. Those short little necks. He remembered the last time he put a breathing tube in a cat in an airway management course. Cats are supposed to be like kids—or was it kids are like cats? He could remember how difficult it was to see the anatomy. It was like looking for a lost ring down a drainpipe.

His heart pounded as he hurried to prepare for the arrival of the emergency medical technicians. Pete could feel the adrenaline rush. He put on latex gloves and hurried to prepare for the worst. As usual, the paramedics underestimated their time of arrival. Normally Pete would be trading jokes with the nurses while they waited. He said little.

An array of stainless steel instruments lay neatly arranged on an adjustable metal stand. Two nurses and a respiratory therapist waited with Pete in the trauma room. Bright beams from the overhead examination lights focused on a flat gurney covered with a pressed white sheet.

EMS whisked a pale Sam Gifford, Jr., a beautiful boy with a perfectly round, bald head, into the trauma room. The paramedic was breathless and almost as pale. Three leads attached to the child's chest ran to a monitor that displayed a flat line. A T-shirt that said "Daddy's Boy" had been cut up the middle and lay tattered at his sides. All this because Sam's older brother had been feeding him grapes that day.

"Doc, we pulled out a grape—still not moving air. Lost the pulse as we pulled up."

"That's OK. Get him on the stretcher so I can take a look. Hand me that laryngoscope."

Like most emergency physicians, Pete had developed a great ability to concentrate in the middle of chaos. Nurses were yelling to the clerk, the phone was ringing, and a crowd of nurses and technicians had gathered to watch the spectacle. He gently placed the metal instrument into Sam's mouth so that he could view the opening to the airway. Cat—my ass, he thought. It didn't look anything like a cat's throat.

"Get me some Magill's."

"Right here, doc."

"Too big. Let me have those hemostats. Son of a gun. This thing is really jammed in there."

Sweat formed on his brow and his glasses fogged; he tossed them onto the instrument tray. Each second that passed made Pete more aware that brain cells would be dying soon. He struggled to get the instrument deep enough into the baby's mouth to grasp the obstructing object. The second slippery green grape proved difficult to extract. It had lodged just above the voice box and was preventing any air from entering the lungs. Two minutes had passed with no pulse. There was no time to think of this boy's parents or to consider how their lives would change if this child died or was brain damaged. In spite of the risk of forcing the grape deeper, Pete pierced it with one side of the instrument. The hemostat stayed in the slimy red grape. He gently grasped and removed it, and then tossed it aside. Without losing sight of the airway, Pete quickly placed a flexible latex tube into the airway to help the blue, lifeless boy breathe.

"Start chest compressions and get an IV going. Put him on a monitor and get some blood drawn. We need a portable chest x-ray right now."

There would be plenty of time later for please and thank you. Pete had nurses and technicians moving in all directions to save Sam. The nurses placed an IV line in one arm. Respiratory therapists taped the tube in place and breathed for the child with a blue vinyl bag attached to oxygen.

"Stop compressions," Pete said. "I've got a pulse. It's too slow. Breathe faster for him. Where is the damn x-ray?"

Sam's pulse gradually returned to normal. The blood pressure was good. The true sign of success, however, was yet to come. Pete knew that they had cut it very close and that the time without oxygen may have been too long. The commotion halted as everyone stood watching the boy. The nurses looked on, brows furrowed. The monitor beeped with each beat. The phone rang in the distance. Pete stood motionless, lightly touching Sam's leg to gauge the quality of the pulse. As the minutes passed, Pete began to wonder if he would be discussing the concept of brain death with the family. Of all the dying people Pete had resuscitated before, never had he wished so much that someone would awaken. Half the time, he was wishing that some of these demented patients, who wouldn't know their own spouse, could be left alone. He doubted very many people would want all of it. What good was it, after all, to be ventilating and chest compressing and cardiac shocking these poor souls? After all the nonagenarians he had resuscitated, you'd think God would look out for this little guy.

As the baby began moving his arms and legs, a great cheer erupted from the medical team. Soon his eyes were open and he was trying to breathe on his own. The tube in his throat prevented him from crying. It would be left in place for an hour or two to be certain that everything was all right. Pete knew from the rapid improvement that all would be fine with the boy. He would be somewhat less optimistic with the parents until more time passed and the tube could be removed. Everyone beamed with joy as Pete slipped out of the room.

Pete made it to the call room before anyone noticed he was on the edge of a full panic attack. His heart pounded, he felt short of breath, and his chest ached. He stripped off the scrub top he was sweating through and sat on the edge of the bed. The panic attacks came less often since he started therapy, but near-death episodes with children got him every time. He ran through Patty Corry's instructions in his head. *Get away from the stimulus. Go to a quiet place. Concentrate on something pleasant. Breathe quietly. Go to that peaceful dimension.* He shivered as the sweat evaporated from his chest. He concentrated to keep the flashbacks at bay while his body responded to the surge of adrenaline. Eventually he would outrun the monster that chased him out of the dark alley.

Gradually his pulse slowed and he breathed easier. He managed to abort a serious attack but each recurrence of panic weakened his confidence that he could ever lick his problem. The fatigue that usually followed these attacks was the part he dreaded most. He knew he would have to get moving. The longer he waited, the harder it would be to get motivated to go back out to see another patient.

"Don't get too comfortable in there, Pete," said the nurse through the door. "EMS is on their way with a 95-year-old from the nursing home in heart failure. And call somebody named Patty. She said you would know what it was about."

She must be clairvoyant.

As Pete walked out of the ER at the end of his 12-hour shift, Dr. Wendel Links intercepted him. Pete could never get the image of a weasel out of his mind whenever he saw the small, thin-lipped man with the perpetual pained expression. Pete wondered if it was hemorrhoids. He noted the trademark bow tie, blue lab coat, and stethoscope around his neck. Pete had known Wendel Links for three years, and the man never called him by his first name. You'd think that out of sheer courtesy the guy would say Peter, Pete, Petey boy, son, buddy, pal, shit head. Anything but Dr. Fredericks.

"Dr. Fredericks, I heard about Sam Griffin. You know I want to hear from you about my patients when they come in."

"I'm sorry Wendel, in the commotion I didn't think anybody got the name of his doctor. I can fill you in now—"

"Never mind," he barked, stopping Pete in mid sentence, "your nurse told me about it." So why didn't you send him by helicopter to Children's Hospital?"

"I felt he was stable to go by ground."

"You need to let me be the judge on cases like this. This will be a good case for us to review at the next pediatric section meeting."

Pete felt like the cat that caught the mouse only to get swatted across the head for bringing it inside the house. He wished he could swat old Wendel over the head. This was the first time in many days that he had something to really feel good about at work. Links managed to ruin it all. Day by day, Pete could feel that Parkview Hospital was sucking the life out of him. He liked seeing the patients, but his job as ER medical director was a source of frustration and resentment. The medical staff frequently put him down and made him feel like an unimportant outsider. His good deeds usually went unrecognized and his failures were thrust in his face. This day, Links had managed to turn a great success into something bad. These insults cut into him. Every time an arrogant physician chastised him, he could hear his father railing about something at their kitchen table.

As Pete grew up, his father rarely offered praise. Criticism, however, was dealt out abundantly. The B+ could have been an A. The triple could have been a homer. He missed some leaves when raking the back yard. Nothing was ever good enough for his father. The only thing that would probably have pleased his father was Pete's graduation from medical school. By that time, he was dead.

Pete sat sulking on the hood of his new white Honda Accord in the hospital parking lot and remembered the message to call Patty Corry. The sun went down beyond scattered clouds as he gazed across the manicured side yard of the hospital. As he pulled his cell phone from his pocket, Pete hoped Patty might elevate his mood.

"I headed off a panic attack after taking care of a sick kid."

"Don't be down about it," Patty said bluntly. "You've come a long way, and our strategy for aborting these attacks seems to be working. Did the child live?"

"Yeah. I pulled him from death's hands," Pete said, feeling a bit better.

"There you go. You need to put the negatives aside. You've got so many positives to think about. Go home and celebrate and kiss your wife."

"I'll do that," Pete said. It amazed him how Patty could turn his mood. Maybe he *was* making progress.

"I almost forgot why I called. Buddy has a conflict. Can we meet at his office a day later?"

"That's fine. I'll see you then. Thanks for being with me."

They said goodnight like old friends do, knowing that the other will always be there. Pete owed his life to Patty. In eighteen months, she had taken him from being emotionally disabled back to full-time work. She saved his career and probably his marriage. Pete would do anything for Patty except tell her that he and Buddy planned to meet alone at 6 a.m. the next day.

CHAPTER 3

▼

Pete pulled in front of Buddy's brownstone on Prospect Street in Georgetown at 6:05 a.m. Two young men in shorts and hooded sweatshirts, university students, jogged past. Little else was happening as the day came alive. Cars lined the curb on both sides of the street. He drummed his fingers on the wheel while he sat blocking his lane. Pete looked forward to spending time with Buddy. They enjoyed a close relationship since meeting six months before. This was not the kind of friendship where two men go to the bar to shoot pool and drink beer twice a month. They had met outside of Buddy's office only twice before, but they spoke on the phone two or three times a week. These interactions had proven to be more beneficial than the sessions in Buddy's office with Patty. They found it easy to open up to each other. They shared their fears, their successes, and their failures. Their respective wives would never believe that either of them was capable of the open and honest exchange of feelings that occurred between them.

Buddy held a University of South Carolina insulated coffee mug in one hand as he closed the heavy wooden door of his part-time home behind him. He walked slowly to Pete's car and groaned as he sat in the passenger seat.

"Hey, Buddy. You OK?"

"Mornin', Pete. My back is givin' me fits lately."

Buddy pulled a sterling silver pill box out of his coat pocket. Pete watched him remove a pale green pill with "OC" imprinted on one side. He recognized it immediately. Buddy downed the pill with a swig of coffee.

"How long you been on the OxyContin?" Pete said in a matter-of-fact way.

"On and off for about a year. I just take 'em when my back is really killin' me."

"Just be careful," Pete said, not wanting to sound patronizing. "You can get hooked pretty quick on those."

"Yeah, I've been warned."

"You ready for this?" Pete said, as he gave Buddy the thumbs up sign.

"I put it off long enough. Let's go. Turn left up there," Buddy said, pointing to the next intersection. "That'll get us to K Street."

They took K to Washington Circle, and then took 23rd past George Washington University Hospital down to the Lincoln Memorial.

"So you've never been to it before?" Pete asked, trying to get Buddy to open up.

"I been down by there for a few ceremonies at the Lincoln Memorial and got close enough to throw a rock at it, but never really went to it like we're gonna do."

"Here's the Lincoln Memorial. Where do I park?"

"Right up there on your right," Buddy said with a grin and a gleam in his eye.

"You're gonna get me towed."

"Naw. You forget who you're ridin' with, son. I'll just put my card under your wiper. Capitol police wouldn't dare." Pete just smiled.

They walked past the Lincoln Memorial and cut over to the Vietnam Veterans Memorial. In silence, they strolled on the brick path next to the polished black granite panels. The dew that had fallen that night reflected the small amount of light that filtered through the fog. Pete felt a chill up his spine as they walked. Buddy stopped at 1967 and studied The Wall. Pete stepped back to lean against a tree on the nearby grass. Buddy expected a flood of memories and flashbacks. Instead, he felt peace and he felt the presence of more than 58,000 soldiers—brothers who sacrificed their youths, their futures, and their dreams. He felt the immense weight of the panels and the gravity of the unfathomable list of the dead and missing. Like every Vietnam Veteran who ever touched his hand to The Wall, Buddy wondered why his name wasn't there.

Buddy searched the panel and found the name. He squatted to read and touch the name of Scott V. Sanders. He ran his fingertips over the carved letters. He barely knew him. Maybe that was better. He wondered if Sanders knew he was sorry. He wondered how much longer he would carry the weight of that panel on his shoulders. Buddy stood and wiped his eyes, then took a few deep breaths. He and Pete walked to the end of the memorial and back.

"Let's go sit with Lincoln for a few minutes," Buddy said, patting Pete on the shoulder.

Mr. Lincoln looked beyond them as they took the steps up. They sat on the top step and looked over the reflecting pool through the fog to the Washington Monument. They said little for about ten minutes.

"I know some of what happened," Buddy said quietly, "but I never heard the whole story."

Pete had told the detailed story of what happened 20 months prior to only a few others. This was a good time to tell it to Buddy.

Like most Saturday evenings, it had been a crazy night at the Parkview Hospital ER. The waiting room overflowed, sick patients lay on stretchers in the hallways, and one of the nurses had called off sick. Drunk patients aggravated the nurses while Pete tried to keep his head above water attending to the ill and injured. Patients and their families waited impatiently in the lobby for hours. Most were hostile by the time Pete could get to them. By 3 a.m., Pete had things under control. He had emptied the lobby and only a few patients remained waiting for test results.

Just about the time Pete hoped to sit down and drink a cup of coffee, Billy Flick came to the triage desk. Billy was an intoxicated, ill-mannered, and unkempt man with a shaved head and a scraggly goatee. The tattoo-to-teeth ratio was quite high for a man in his 30's. He sported the obligatory love and hate jailhouse tattoos on his knuckles along with multiple others on his arms and torso. His surprisingly clean girlfriend and their two-year-old daughter, Dusty, accompanied him. Sharon had threatened to leave if Billy did not do something about his drinking problem. Billy demanded to be seen promptly or he would leave. The natural inclination of any triage nurse who had just suffered through an evening with a jam-packed lobby would be to say, "Don't let the door hit your fat ass on the way out." Instead, she brought them back to a room and rolled her eyes at Pete as she walked back out to the triage desk. Pete looked over the chart and went to the room. Billy sat on the stretcher with his arms crossed. Pete introduced himself and asked how he could help them.

Initially there was no response, then Sharon quietly said, "Billy is here because he drinks too much."

Pete looked at Billy and said, "Tell me about that."

"If she says so," Billy snorted, as he folded his leather jacket across his lap.

"Come on, baby, you said you'd do this for me. I can't do this any more with you if you're gonna drink," Sharon said, through tears, as she shifted Dusty on her lap.

"You ain't leavin'," Billy challenged.

"I will, Billy. I'm serious this time."

"Why don't we get back to seeing what we can do to help you," Pete said, trying to keep the peace.

Billy's face turned red and he clenched his fists. If he were a dog, his ears would have been pulling back and the hair on his back bristling.

"There ain't no helpin' me. And you ain't leavin'," Billy said as he glared at Sharon and pulled a .38 caliber revolver from his coat.

Pete instinctively scooted his chair back to the door. The terrified look on Sharon's face as she tried to shield her daughter etched permanently into Pete's brain right then. Before he could take a breath, Billy shot both Sharon and Dusty in the head. Blood spattered half the room. Sharon slumped against the wall and Dusty dropped to the floor. Their blood flowed together into a maroon pond of despair in the middle of the room. Pete's ears rang from the loud pop of the gun. It was just as well that he didn't hear the dull thud when Dusty hit the floor. Pete sat in disbelief, mouth agape and eyes wide. Rage showed in Billy's bloodshot eyes as he yelled profanities at his dying girlfriend. The acrid smell of the gunpowder engulfed the room.

"God. Let me help them," Pete pleaded with Billy.

"Sit still and shut up. They're dead anyway."

Pete could hear commotion and several screams outside the room. A nurse called in to see what was happening. "Are you OK, Dr. Fredericks?"

"No. Listen. Get everyone out of this ER right now—fast as you can."

"But Dr. Fr-"

"Go. Get out now."

There were more screams as the blood ran under the door. Billy pointed the gun at Pete's face.

"How 'bout you come with us, doc?" Billy hissed.

Pete thought quickly of a way to respectfully decline to die with Billy. "Who's going to tell your story?"

Billy thought for a moment and pulled back his weapon. As he pointed it under his chin, he said, "I don't hear you telling me to put this gun down."

Pete could tell Billy was having second thoughts and was trying to muster the courage to do it. He had no desire to help Billy. He wanted him to get it over with. Billy clenched his teeth. Pete said nothing. Billy fired.

Buddy rested his hand on Pete's shoulder. "I'm always right here with you."

They walked to Pete's car and he dropped Buddy at his office. Before getting out, Buddy handed Pete a paper with a name and a number. "I talked to a good friend of mine on Hilton Head Island this week. This is the name of the CEO of the hospital. They're lookin' for a new director for the ER. You should call him and check it out."

"This sounds great," Pete said enthusiastically. "I don't want to offend you, but I'd rather that you not go to bat for me on this. If I get the job, I want to know it was because I'm qualified."

"That's fine with me. You let me know if you want my help."

Pete's mind raced all the way home. He had been itching to leave Parkview and this was his ticket out. He had enough of the provincial medical staff and the outdated facility. He also wouldn't miss the D.C. area traffic.

CHAPTER 4

▼

Pete pulled in the drive at his smart-looking red Cape Cod style home in Rockville completely unprepared to discuss relocation with his wife. A tall wooden fence bordered the small back yard where daffodils and hostas would bloom in beds along the fence. His and Molly's Irish Setter, Sean, loped across the yard to meet him. Pete yelled a stern "Off" to prevent Sean from jumping up and soiling his pants. Then he scratched him behind the ears. He could smell paint thinner.

He walked around to the wooden deck where he found Molly and planted a wet kiss on her lips. He spread his arms in an exaggerated way to avoid touching the yellow paint splatters that covered most of her slender body and oval face.

"Do you want me to hose you off out here or inside?" Pete teased as he ran his hand through her long blond hair. "Did any of this paint make it to the walls?"

"Yeah, you should see it," Molly said, blue eyes beaming. "The bathroom looks great. This was the last thing to do inside. Except for the garage, we are done."

For Pete, this was good and bad news. The novelty of the remodeling had worn off long before, so he was happy to have an end to the mess. The dust, the moving furniture from room to room, and construction supplies all around the house made Pete wish they had purchased new construction. On the other hand, Molly was rooted like an old oak in their home. She had invested so much of herself that the task of convincing her to relocate would be daunting.

Pete knew that Molly felt a great sense of satisfaction and pride in their home. When they purchased the house two years before, it may as well have been condemned. The roof leaked, the decor was fit for a bus station lobby, and the appliances were all avocado green. The first task had been to gut the place and start over. Taking on one room at a time, Molly had slowly transformed it into one of those houses that appear in *Colonial Homes Magazine.* All but the trees had been removed from the yard, and new landscaping, sod, front walk, and two-rail fence were placed. The neighbors were ecstatic to see the neighborhood ugly duckling become a beautiful swan. Except for the plumbing and electrical work, Molly did the work and served as the general contractor. Molly's father was a general contractor and she had learned plenty about home construction working summers with him.

If Pete was ever going to get Molly to go along with a move, he'd have to have a plan—a plan to which he had given little thought.

"It's hard to believe what this house has become. You should take some time to do something fun now," he ventured.

"This is my fun."

"I know you love this. I just thought you might want to pick up your clubs again."

"Actually I have been thinking of taking up golf again. Dad would love it."

"It's funny that you should mention golf. Sit down and put up your feet. Interesting news today."

"Oh, yeah. How did it go with Buddy?"

"He's great," Pete said avoiding giving any details to Molly about Buddy. He took a deep breath and decided to just plunge right in. "Buddy told me about a directorship opportunity on Hilton Head Island. He has friends on the island. It sounds promising and I want to check it out. I don't know any details right now but I am going to talk to the CEO and find out more. What do you think we could get for the house?"

The pause was so pregnant, it could have delivered twins. Molly sat and stared into space. Pete shifted in his seat as sweat formed under his shirt.

"You're going way too fast here. We've never even talked about moving and you have the house on the market already," Molly said, as she stood from the wrought iron deck chair. "I know that you're not happy at work, but do you really want to uproot us right now? We've done all this work on the house, plus I can't leave my dad. I'm all he's got. What if he gets sick like Mom did?"

Pete had done this before and now regretted not remembering previous lessons. He had the bad habit of forgetting about other people when he was excited about something. This tunnel vision had caused previous arguments and Pete knew that he was not helping his cause with his current blunder.

"I'm sorry. I shouldn't have dumped this in your lap like that," Pete said as he sat on the wood bench that bordered the deck.

"I understand that you're excited, but won't there be a long line of people vying for a job in paradise?"

"Sure, but they don't want some washed-up surgeon who is winding down his career. They want someone who is young and energetic."

"I can understand why this looks attractive. I just have a lot of reservations about moving. You know I want to be near my dad. Please don't get upset. We need to talk about this. I feel like we are finally settled in," Molly said, voice cracking.

Pete wanted to put off having children until they were more settled. He knew Molly felt the time was right and that South Carolina would be another excuse to delay starting a family. Molly stepped down to the edge of the grass. She turned back to look at Pete.

"You can't run from your problems."

"This is not about Billy Flick," Pete said angrily.

She didn't mean to do it, but Molly unintentionally touched a raw nerve. She thought he was getting better. What she didn't know was the event still invaded his thoughts and poisoned his sleep. Pete rarely brought it up because of the pain it caused. It helped to talk to Buddy about it, but any discussion with Molly just made it worse.

"Damn it. This could be really good for us."

"No, it sounds more like it would be good for *you*. Where do I fit in this picture? You need to think about that," Molly said as she walked back onto the deck. "We can't just pull up stakes like this," she said more calmly. She sat down again next to Pete and put her arm around his shoulders. "I'm sorry I made you angry."

"I'm not angry," Pete said, embarrassed that it set him off.

"Yes you are. Let's think about it and talk more later."

Pete spent the day making notes and thinking about Hilton Head Island. He and Molly had been to Kiawah Island near Charleston, but had never been to Hilton Head. He had heard great things about the beaches and the gated communities known as plantations. Fond memories of trips to the South Carolina shore were alive in his mind. He loved exploring and fishing in the tidal streams. The soft white sand and grand beauty of the Atlantic shore made him long to return.

It was a restless night for Pete. Thoughts of a new professional challenge and living on a subtropical island filled his head. He dreamed of swimming in the warm ocean, searching for a home, and fishing. The warm ocean breezes and the prospect of a new start with a new medical staff had him mentally packing his bags already.

CHAPTER 5

▼

Senator Buddy Duke walked toward his office with his chief of staff, Dick Coswell, at his side. After several weeks of cold and damp weather on the Potomac, the unseasonably warm winter day brightened his outlook. Ten years away from the mild South Carolina winters did nothing to thicken his blood. Knowing that he was done with meetings for the week, he loosened his tie as they walked. Buddy wondered why he wasted time going to the Appropriations Committee meetings. All the deals were cut in the majority leader's office anyway. If they televised the meeting, it might be worth it. He knew that he would need to have more face time on television if he was to make a viable run for the presidency.

"Do we have a commitment from the network about 'Meet the Press' for Sunday?" Buddy said as he shot a grin at the officer who was guarding the Russell Senate Office Building.

"We need to go over their topic before we commit," Dick Coswell said casually, as if talking about a school debate.

"I don't really care what their damn topic is. I'm gonna get my sound bites in no matter what they want to jaw about. So what is it anyway?" Duke nodded politely to the senator from Oklahoma, whom he considered to be a back-stabbing weasel. He was ever thankful they belonged to the same party.

"National Health Care. Van Horn's got a big boner for getting it back in the spotlight."

"Hell, those idiots have memories like my five-year-old grandkid. Do the Hillary fiasco and the insurance company ads ring any bells over there?" Not expecting a reply, he continued without a breath. "Shit, it don't matter. I'm gonna soft step the whole thing and get my licks in about jobs. That's all anybody really cares about anyway."

"Just don't say anything about healthcare they can pin you down on later." More than most people in his position, Coswell took a very familiar tone with Buddy. They couldn't be more familiar if they were related. Vietnam made them brothers in the bonds of blood and deceit.

"Who else is on with me?"

"Carson from California."

"God, he'll be so hung over, he won't put two rational thoughts together. And make sure I get a makeup person who doesn't make me look embalmed this time. And no fags. That last one made my hair stand on end. Gimme an all-American girl that'll make my dick stand on end."

They bid good bye to the secretaries and staffers leaving for the weekend and settled into Duke's office. Coswell closed the door.

"Get you a drink?"

"The usual."

Coswell clinked ice into two Clemson University highball glasses and poured three fingers of Kentucky Bourbon into each. "Contributions from Hilton Head are late this month. You want me to make a call?"

"Give it another week or so. It's hard to believe that Bennett had me kissing his short little ass all these years and now he's my damn lap dog. Thirty-seven years it's been. You ever think we'd be sittin' here with me in the most exclusive political fraternity on earth?"

"You've come a long way."

"I'll always have you to thank, Dick." Duke walked to get a refill after emptying his glass. He put his hand on Coswell's shoulder as he passed. "Don't worry about Hilton Head, Bennett won't cross me."

CHAPTER 6

▼

Clay Stevens reclined in a high-backed leather chair and pondered the situation in his ER. He stretched his long legs across the corner of the desk in his modest office at Hilton Head Hospital. His gaunt face gazed out the window at a small lagoon where a 10-foot alligator sunned himself on the bank. Azaleas skirted one bank, and an ancient live oak tree spread its creeping branches over the opposite bank. A light breeze drifted in from a side window. This office was much smaller than the one he occupied in Charleston, but he would never trade his current view through the large picture window.

Clay had vacationed on Hilton Head many times and always dreamed of retiring there. When the job of CEO for the hospital opened, it was an easy decision for him. He didn't mind the reduction in pay and didn't miss the care of a big house and yard. He purchased a condominium near the marina and a fishing boat. He took every chance to throw a line in the water. Life was good for Clay, but the job was tougher than he thought it would be. He didn't anticipate dealing with harsh medical staff politics as he had in the large hospital in Charleston, and he was given little warning about the depth of the controversy with Dr. Wilhelm Betts. In spite of all his problems, Clay remained excited about the challenges and held high hopes for great improvement in emergency services at the hospital.

Clay puffed on a cigar as he wrestled with how to present the problem of Dr. Betts to his latest candidate for ER director. Normally he liked to leave discussion of sticky problems for late in the interview process. He'd already lost a good candidate who became spooked over the Betts issue, so he wanted to ease into the topic without making Pete alarmed. Clay wanted to be fair and up front but, at the same time, knew that his current ER group would be leaving in four months. He needed someone in place before the group left, and time was running short. Colonoscopy would be preferable to last-minute scrambling for weekend ER coverage.

He picked up the phone and punched in Pete's number. After making their introductions and apologies for missing calls, Clay got right down to business.

"This is a great opportunity here," he said in his gentlemanly South Carolina accent. "I don't think I'd be exaggerating to say this is a once in a lifetime deal. I'm looking for an energetic emergency doc to take over my ER and bring in a solid group. I looked over the fax you sent, and it looks like you're that kinda person."

"That's a nice compliment," Pete said, a little hesitant to toot his own horn.

"I see that you list fishing as a hobby."

"I enjoy fresh-water fishing but haven't done too much in salt water."

"This here is the place to come if you want to do some great fishing. Yesterday morning, I caught three redfish and two white bass. One red was two feet—not those pecker-length fresh-water fish. Those reds fight like a damn shark. Why don't you come on down here and take a look around? Maybe we'll catch a few fish, too."

Clay went on to explain the merits of the hospital and the island. He talked up safety, good schools, great climate, and easy pace of life. He skipped discussion of the yearly threat of hurricanes and how isolating it can be to live on a small island away from larger cities. The opulence and sophistication of the island were a big plus, but it still lived like a small town. Clay liked it that way, but he also knew that candidates were used to better shopping than Belks and Wal-Mart, and more sporting events than the yearly golf tournament.

Clay concluded that Pete was swallowing the hook and he had plenty of time to set it later. He could proceed with the obligatory warning about Betts. With any luck, Pete would forget about it anyway.

"Before I let you go, I want to fill you in on something. We're having a spittin' match over one of the members of the medical staff. Wilhelm Betts is a cancer doctor who practices on the edge of conventional oncology. He takes on patients who have been written off by other doctors. He makes treatment decisions based on certain DNA sequences in the tumors. Nobody else in the country is doing this, so the medical staff is uptight about it. He seems like a good enough gent. I'm no doctor—I don't know a proctoscope from a stethoscope—so I don't know if there's any problem or not. I just want you to know if you get the job here, you'll sit on the Executive Committee and will be dealing with this."

After hanging up, he paced the floor. Pete felt he had already established good chemistry with Clay and they would hit it off when they met. His argument with Molly quickly receded. Pete was nagged, though, about why Clay would bring up something about another doctor so early in the interview process. He knew that quality issues usually get handled privately by medical staffs, and little public fuss is created. In his experience, doctors usually wanted to keep a quality issue more quiet than some dark family secret. Why would there be a problem? Well, whatever it was, he figured it couldn't be anything bad enough to prevent his move to paradise.

CHAPTER 7

▼

Dr. Wilhelm Betts reviewed pathology results in his office at Hilton Head Hospital while he wolfed down pastrami on wheat. His unkempt thin gray hair dangled across his ruddy face as he leaned over to eat. This meal as well as many others could have been skipped. His 300-pound frame barely fit into his swivel chair. He wiped his mouth on yesterday's napkin as the phone rang.

"Betts here."

"Dr. Betts, this is Christine calling from Washington, D.C. Do you have a moment for Senator Duke?"

"Always I have time for my good friend the senator. Please put him up."

Betts, a German immigrant, still had some difficulty with the nuances of the English language. Considering where he started, though, he had done quite well. Betts arrived by ship as a young man in 1960 with the help of a benevolent grandfather. He learned English, graduated college, and went on to medical school and residency. Two years before, he moved his practice to Hilton Head with the support of Buddy Duke.

"Wilhelm, how are you, friend?"

"Just fine, Buddy. Busy, busy, busy."

"Good." Buddy wasn't quite sure how to approach the subject. He knew Betts was sensitive and didn't want to set him off. "Tell me what's happenin' with these questions about your practice."

"I have meeting tomorrow with Stevens, hospital CEO, and Dr. Daniels, new president of medical staff. I know more after that."

"You keep me posted. I'll be down to see ya'll next week. You take care 'til then."

"OK, we'll eat big steak dinner and have French wine."

Betts pushed his sandwich to the side and shifted uneasily in his chair. He had the same sick feeling he had when he was about to lose his privileges at the hospital in New York City. This time, he hoped he could do a better job convincing the medical staff that he was on the cutting edge of cancer treatment and not the outer fringe. He also hoped that having the support of a United States senator this time would keep him out of trouble. All he wanted to do was run his lab and treat patients.

His afternoon patients were arriving and already he was running 20 minutes behind. He lumbered to the first of four examination rooms and picked up the chart of Emily Carter, a 58-year-old with metastatic pancreatic cancer. At their first encounter, Betts had ordered multiple blood tests, magnetic resonance scans of the brain, chest, and abdomen, and a needle biopsy of the tumor that had spread to the liver. This tissue was analyzed in Betts' private lab using an expensive and lucrative process.

"Good afternoon, Mr. and Mrs. Carter. I'm sorry to be late. I had to take important call from Senator Duke."

Betts had come highly recommended to the Carters so he knew they already held him in high regard. He had also established excellent rapport on their first visit. The fact that he was just conversing with a senator would be all the more impressive.

"Have you found a comfortable place to stay?"

"Yes, doctor," Mr. Carter said. "There's a nice motel at mid-island that is very reasonable this time of year."

"Good. You let my staff know how we help you while you're here. OK, since we met three weeks ago, I learn very much about your body and how it is fighting pancreatic cancer. We already know it is in your liver and some lymph nodes— that is bad but is no surprise. It has not spread more. The MRI of head and chest are OK—that is good. Here is interesting part. We checked DNA of your tumor and it has sequence of DNA like other tumors that I treat before with success."

Betts knew his DNA theory was unproven. He had a growing number of cases but only a few successes. He hoped to publish a report when he had more cases. He justified the fact that he was experimenting without permission because almost all of his patients had been told they were terminal but would not give up. He offered a chance for a cure—even if it was a small chance. He offered hope.

Emily's eyes brightened. "When can we start?" she asked.

"In two days, you start your trip back to good health, Emily. I and my staff will be right with you and husband all of way. Remember, I don't give up unless you tell me. Tomorrow, my staff spends about four hours with you teaching about chemotherapy. We will see how you are doing with special diet and exercise plan I started on your last visit, and we will put in a special IV for giving chemo."

"Oh, I'm thrilled. I can't wait to get started. Thank you so much, Dr. Betts." Her furrowed brow had vanished.

"You thank me by getting better, Emily."

"I know this is an uncomfortable topic for all of us," Mr. Carter said. "But, I need to ask you about the finances of this."

Betts knew the Carters lived a comfortable life in Pennsylvania but did not have large sums of cash on hand. He knew they would most likely have to sell off some assets and dip into life insurance policies or mortgage the house to pay for the treatment. Their health insurance would cover only a fraction of the cost.

"Yes, I don't like to talk about money either," Betts said somberly. "As we talked three weeks ago, billing office asks for upfront payments of $10,000 at a time, as we go. Insurance company should pay you back some of it. We help you with that. I cannot tell you how much total will be."

"Let's get started then," Mr. Carter said, in the most upbeat voice he could muster.

"Good. Now I sit here with you and answer every question you have until we are done," Betts said as he reached to hold Emily's hand.

CHAPTER 8

▼

Pete was not looking for trouble when he went to work the next evening, but it found him soon after he arrived. Mark Dickman—an appropriate name, Pete thought—was waiting to pounce. Dickman was one of three general surgeons who wielded considerable power with the Parkview medical staff and with the hospital administration. He was not to be crossed if it could be avoided. Pete had taken his share of tongue lashings and had no interest in another one. This situation, however, could not be avoided. One of Dickman's partners had come to the ER one night in a drunken state to see a patient. Pete had closed his eyes to a lot of bad behavior over the years, knowing that patient care was not really affected. Verbal abuse of doctors and nurses, throwing charts, and incessant complaining were just part of the background noise of his work life. But this was not something he could ignore. He felt an obligation to protect patients from a physician who may have been incompetent, if only temporarily. He also had a genuine desire to see any impaired physician get help. He did not enjoy being the rat, but to look away was more objectionable. He had to go with his instincts—this was not part of the ethics curriculum in medical school. Since Pete had brought the problem to the attention of the chief of the medical staff, Dickman was there to skewer him over the whole thing. Dickman waited for him outside the call room and out of earshot from the nursing station.

"You think you're pretty smart," Dickman fumed.

"Pardon me?"

"You know what I'm talking about, Fredericks. You wanna play hard ball?"

"No I don't. I raised a legitimate quality issue through proper channels. Am I supposed to ignore this type of thing?"

"Damn right. You listen up. Stay the hell out of my business or I'll be in yours."

"Look, I don't appreciate your threats. I didn't ask for your alcoholic partner to stink up my ER that night, but now I'm stuck with it. Get out of my face or we'll be in Executive Committee talking about *you.*"

"So that's the way you want it. Your days are numbered here, pal."

Dickman stormed off. Pete had seen him blow a gasket before so he wasn't going to sweat it. He knew that as a medical director he would have his nose bloodied on occasion. He was tired of getting slugged and not fighting back, though. It felt good to pile some of the crap back onto Dickman. Pete knew that this exchange would have him in hot water with the CEO. He would have to deal with that when the time came. This was just one of many unhappy encounters he would not miss if he could land the job on Hilton Head. Pete had bigger fish to fry anyway. He needed to find a way to convince Molly that the Carolina coast beckoned her. He thought he might get Molly's father to move with them. Golf would be a plus for Molly and, it seemed to him, it would be a great place to raise kids. What kid wouldn't want to grow up by the beach? There must be a few fixer-uppers on the island. He had all the arguments lined up for the next time they talked.

By 3 a.m. there were no more patients to see, so Pete lay down in the call room. At 5, he was awakened by a frantic call from Molly. He knew there was trouble because she rarely called him at work and never in the middle of the night.

"Pete, I'm scared. Someone broke a window downstairs. Sean's going berserk. What should I do?"

"Is somebody in the house?"

"I don't know."

"Be calm and do these things quickly. Lock yourself and Sean in the bedroom and push the dresser past the edge of the door. Call 911. Call me back as soon as you get off the phone with the police."

Pete hated being away from home at night, but felt better with Sean there. While Molly called the police, he made arrangements for someone to come in early for him. He couldn't leave until another doctor arrived, and it was killing him to wait. Once his relief arrived, Pete sprinted home.

Molly was sitting with a police officer in the living room. Nobody had entered their home. A front window pane had been broken and shards of glass were scattered across the expensive Persian rug on the living room floor. A baseball wrapped in a plastic evidence bag sat on the coffee table. Pete kept the incident with Dickman to himself. This had to be some kids from a few blocks over. He thought Dickman was a psycho but not crazy enough to do this. After the police left, he consoled Molly while they sat together on the living room couch. Even though he was concerned, he couldn't help but think this was a unique opportunity to make his case about moving. He'd have to be subtle or Molly would see through it and the punishment for that could last for days.

"I love this house as much as you do, Mol. But you know this neighborhood's got problems. We've got a lot of rental housing over by the interstate. Sooner or later, it's going to affect our property values. And neither of us feels very safe right now. We need to think about this for when we have kids. We have to think about our investment and our safety. If I were a kid, I'd rather grow up by the beach than four blocks over from the interstate."

Molly got up and began to pace the floor, avoiding the broken glass.

"I just finished all this work," she said raising her arms in the air. "I'd like to stay and enjoy it for a while. Don't you think this was just a prank?"

"Yeah, it could be the Johnson's pack of brats. For all we know, they're on crack. Why else would they be up in the middle of the night? If there is enough of this kind of thing, people will start moving out. You don't want to be the last one left on the street, do you?"

No answer, but Pete thought maybe he was making some headway. There was no reason to pile on, but he needed reinforcements.

"Your dad is always level headed about this kind of thing. Let's get him over here so he can help us think about this."

Molly's father arrived in time for doughnuts and coffee. He brought a piece of glass, a glass cutter, and window glaze. Roy Albertson was a take-charge kind of man. He approached his business and his life in a no-nonsense proactive style. Pete thought that, at times, he could be a bit overbearing but, for the most part, they got along well. He valued Roy's opinion and Roy was always eager to give it. Pete explained the problem with the neighborhood, the baseball through the window, and then revealed the Hilton Head opportunity.

"It's funny how these neighborhoods can change. Sometimes it happens slowly; other times there's a mad dash to either sell houses or rent them out. As soon as the renters come in, you're screwed. I think you two need to think hard about getting out of this house on your own terms. It's not hopeless. There's an upside with this Hilton Head deal. Go get the job. If I had the opportunity to build homes there when I was your age, there's no question about what I'd have done. That's a fine place to live."

"Daddy, I can't leave you here by yourself. Now that Mom's gone, who's going to look after you if you get sick?"

"Nonsense. I'm fine. I'm not dying of cancer or anything else anytime soon. I'll be down there so often to play golf, you'll be trying to get rid of me. Maybe I'll just get a condo on the beach. Yeah, then I can come and go as I please. So it's settled. Pete flies down there to get the job, we sell the house, and then we find a nice place down there."

CHAPTER 9

▼

Sixty-five degrees felt balmy. A light breeze sifted through the palmetto bushes. Pete wished he had a hammock to stretch out in. The muscular man wore forest green coveralls with the name "Walt" stitched above the pocket. He approached Pete as he waited to hail a cab in front of the terminal. Walt appeared to be quite fit for a man of 61.

"You may wait some time for a cab, if you're lookin' for one," Walt said, his deep voice resonating above the sound of a plane in the background.

"I guess I don't have much choice. Do you have any suggestions?"

"I do. By the way, I'm Walt Ferguson."

"Pleasure to meet you, Mr. Ferguson. Name's Pete."

"No need to be so formal, doc," Walt said, as he adjusted his tortoise-shell glasses on his face.

"How'd you know I'm a doctor?"

"Clay Stevens told me a young doctor would be comin' to the island today to interview for the ER job. Last name is Fredericks, right?"

"Right again. I just flew in from-"

"Maryland." An easy smile spread across Walt's face and his wise eyes gleamed.

"Man, Walt, I can't tell you much, can I?"

"Sure you can. I'm just messin' with you."

"How do you know Clay?"

"I run the maintenance department at the hospital. Clay and I fish together every once in a while. He supplies the boat and I find the good spots. Don't let that ol' buzzard tell you otherwise."

Without realizing it, Pete fell into easy conversation with Walt, as if they were friends who just saw each other the week before. Normally, Pete took a while to warm up to people, but Walt's casual and inviting way made him feel instantly welcome.

"I bet you've fished every stream and flat around Hilton Head," Pete said, as he put a foot up on a bench.

"I've done my share of fishin', that's for sure. I never tire of it. Even as a boy, when we fished to eat, I enjoyed it."

"Were you born here?"

"Sure was. And my mama, too." Walt sat on the bench and extended his palm to offer Pete a seat. He leaned back and crossed his legs at the ankles. This gave Pete the feeling that Walt's sole purpose in life that morning was to sit, talk, and make him feel welcome. Pete's busy pace of life offered him little time to sit, talk, and allow time to pass. This was like a cool breeze across his back on a hot day.

"Tell me about your family."

"Mama's great granddad came here to work the cotton and we've been here since. Three of my six brothers and sisters are here. My youngest brother, Paul, is a doctor in Atlanta. My two older sisters passed on. Two of my brothers, Douglas and Grier, own a gas station and convenience store. My closest brother, Denny, is slow. He lives with mama and helps her."

"Did you ever think about leaving?"

"Oh, every once in a while when I was young, I thought about it. My daddy died young, so I reckoned it'd be best to stay and be with my family. I have no regrets, Pete. I love Hilton Head. Rich folks work their whole lives to retire here. I must be the richest man on the island getting to live here my whole life." Walt stood and lifted Pete's bag. "There's no sense in waitin' for a cab. I'll take you to the hospital, if you don't mind riding in the hospital's pickup truck. I just made a quick trip over here to pick up a part for the generator. We lose power all the time out here. I'll give you the islander's tour and have you to the hospital in plenty of time."

"That sounds good to me, but I don't want to take you away from your work."

"Haven't spent much time in the South, have you? Relax, I got the whole day to get this part installed."

The new friends made their way to Walt's white pickup. Pete tossed his bag into the bed of the well-maintained truck. As they turned onto the main road, the beauty and simplicity of the common areas amazed him. Palms, palmettos, and flowering bushes accented the spacious median of the boulevard. There were no billboards, no neon signs, no golden arches, and no visible telephone or electric lines. No sign stood taller than six feet. The manicured landscape looked better than Pete's own back yard. The elaborate entrances to the various plantations invited his curiosity.

Walt turned down a dirt road and traveled half a mile through dense woods, stopping at a clearing behind a dune. Pete marveled at the untouched beauty. The green spartina grass, which sprouted from the wetlands and bordered the tidal streams, swayed with the sea breeze. They walked a weathered wooden path over the sand dune to the beach. Two herons gently lifted from their perch on a log and winged off to a nearby marsh. A cormorant, perched on a piling with his wings outstretched in the sun, remained.

"This here's the best beach on Hilton Head. Most folks use the other public beaches where there's good parking. If you sit here a spell, you'll see a dozen types of birds, sand crabs, stingrays, and dolphin. In the early morning, you might even see deer. This is where the sea turtles lay their eggs. The lights near the developed areas confuse the turtles so they come here."

"How's the water for swimming, Walt?"

"It's cold this time of year but, come June, the beach will be full of swimmers."

"Any sharks?"

"Oh yeah, plenty. I've caught lots of 'em. They don't bother the swimmers, though. Never heard of any shark bite. Never heard of any gator bitin' nobody either."

"There's alligators?"

Pete felt like he was on a private nature tour. *Alligators. Awesome. Where do I sign up for this deal?*

"Sure, Pete. The lagoons are full of them. Last I heard, two thousand of them live here. Don't bother nobody. Just don't let your dog run. Come on. I want to show you something else."

They turned around and headed back toward Route 278 and headed north past Hilton Head Plantation. They turned right onto Squire Pope Road until they found a dusty and bumpy road that they followed to a clearing where a Low Country style home stood.

"These live oaks are the oldest trees on the island, Pete. They survived the great hurricane of 1893. They were probably here long before the Civil War. Now, this house here belonged to my late Aunt Verbena. Her husband and kids are gone, so she willed it to mama. This is a much nicer place than hers and it looks over the waterway, too. Mama says she's not movin'. There must be two acres and a dozen old live oaks. I can't understand why she doesn't want to move here. I guess she's just set in her ways. None of us wants to buy it, so we are listing it with a realtor once we clean it up. Come inside with me. I need to get something while we're here."

Even though Pete left all the remodeling to Molly, some of her knowledge rubbed off on him. He noticed how brick foundation supports, hidden by latticework, elevated the house six feet. This hammered in the idea that he would have to live with the threat of flooding during hurricane season. Broad wooden front steps led to a deep front porch with a swing and three wooden rockers. The steep-pitched tin roof had no gutters. A brick chimney stood at one end and white clapboard covered the exterior. He liked the elegant simplicity of the structure. Peeling green storm shutters, designed to close to protect the windows, hung in disrepair and served as another reminder of tropical weather. The simple floor plan consisted of a center hall, kitchen, dining room, parlor, and living room down and three bedrooms and a bath up. The back porch provided a panoramic view of the marsh and the Intracoastal Waterway. This view alone would make Pete endure another big remodel job. A small shed in the side yard seemed close to collapsing under its own weight.

"Feel free to look around, Pete."

"When was this house built?"

"Probably near the turn of the century. Few buildings survived the big storm. My granddad told stories to make the hair on your neck stand on end. Hours of wind and rain battered Hilton Head. The tide ran right over all but the north end of the island. Thousands drowned. It's a miracle that any of my kin survived it. Let's walk down to the pier. I can remember crabbing from this pier with my cousins like it was last week. I cherish those simple days when all my brothers and sisters were together. We'd jump off the pier and swim on hot days. My cousin Johnny went swimming here one night and drowned. They found his body near the ferry launch three days later. That was before they built the bridge."

The history of the house and Walt's family intrigued Pete. Having been adopted as an infant when his parents were killed in an accident, he knew no blood relatives. His sheltered upbringing as an only child seemed strange compared to the joy Walt described growing up around this house. Pete's family experience left him with a jaded view of family life. His parents' loveless marriage and his father's distant and harsh attitude toward him left a scar on Pete's soul. Yet hearing stories from people such as Walt made him wonder.

"You've known a lot of loss in your life, haven't you?"

"I guess so. I don't really dwell on it."

"You seem to be at peace with the world. I've seen plenty of people who have lived lives much easier than yours, Walt. They are angry and depressed folks. You seem very content."

"I thank the Lord every day for my life. God's peace is in me. It helps me to gratefully accept what He gives me and understandingly give up what He takes back. His grace shines on me. I consider myself a blessed and lucky man."

Clay Stevens discussed a new complaint about the ER on the phone as Pete entered the office. After introductions, they sat in wing chairs in the corner. As he settled in, Pete admired a large trout mounted on the wall behind the desk.

"Walt's a great guy," Clay said.

"Yes, indeed. I truly enjoyed talking to him."

"Good. You'll see him again this afternoon."

"Is Walt coming to lunch?"

"Sure is. You don't mind going fishing, do you? You can change before we go."

"Fishing is just fine," Pete said, excited about fishing but at the same time perplexed about Clay's casual approach to things.

"How was your flight?"

"No problems. I enjoyed seeing the island from the air."

"First time here, right?"

"Yes. I had to find the island on the map."

"That's fine. We'll make sure you get the big tour of the island. You'll spend a few hours tomorrow afternoon with Rick Dawson. Rick's sort of a free spirit, but he knows this island. He'll give you good advice on properties. What do you think of Hilton Head so far?"

"Very nice. Everything is so clean and green. I'm eager to get back into some of the neighborhoods."

"Plantations."

"Right, plantations."

"What would your wife think of livin' on Hilton Head? It's Molly, right?"

"Yes. I'm not sure. She has just finished restoring our house in Maryland and her family and friends are there. We'll have to see."

"Well, let's head out. The tide is starting to move."

Clay gave part of his canned tour of the island on the way with some island history thrown in. He turned down a dirt road and headed toward the marina. Clay took great pride in his 20-foot Carolina Skiff. The flat bottom made it perfect for inland fishing. A deep blue Bimini top provided shade for the sharp-looking craft. Walt stowed gear on the boat as the two approached.

"Hey, Walt. I'm glad to see you're coming with us."

"Pete, if you want to catch fish, I *got* to come."

"Don't let this old coot tell you any fish stories. It was me who found the spot where Walt caught that 35-inch red last week."

"Yeah, even a blind squirrel finds a nut every once in a while."

"Walt, don't you have some work to do?" kidded Clay.

"He can dish it out but he can't take it. Let's quit jawin' and get goin' while the tide's on the move."

"Don't we need to buy some bait first?" Pete asked.

"I never bought bait in my life. We're gonna catch our bait and I'm gonna show you how," Walt said proudly.

The three cast off from the pier and sped up the Intracoastal Waterway. Clay turned up a tidal stream on the mainland side, putting the engine in neutral while the skiff coasted. Walt untangled a pale blue nylon net and attached its rope to his wrist. Pete had never seen such a contraption. Walt motioned to Clay to stop the boat. Clay touched the throttle into reverse several times. Walt held part of the net bunched in one hand. In his mouth and in the other outstretched hand, he held the edge of the net. Ahead of the bow, Pete could see the murky water turning as if it were at a low boil. Walt turned his body and, in one easy motion, tossed the net off the bow. The centrifugal force caused the net to fan out into a circle. It landed flat on the water with a quiet whoosh and sank to the bottom. Walt quickly pulled the rope, causing the net to bunch at the end. He lifted it into the boat and tossed the net, which was spattered with bits of decaying spartina grass, onto the floor of the boat near the live well. Clay opened the live well and Walt dumped a dozen wiggling mullet into it.

"It's much harder than it looks, Pete. The last time I tried to throw the net, I fell overboard. Walt laughed so hard, he almost fell in with me. I've been practicing in my yard but I just can't get the motion. It must be a black thing. What do you think, Walt?"

"Nah, you're just uncoordinated, Clay. It's all in the hips. Let's go to that spot you found last week."

Walt cut bait while they skimmed south. Pete helped to prepare the rods and pulled the anchor from the hold in the bow. The three enjoyed a beautiful afternoon of fishing, deli sandwiches, and conversation. They moved to five different spots but there was no luck. Around 3 p.m., storm clouds billowed in the south. Distant thunder rolled along the shoreline. As the sun slipped behind the clouds, the colors became more vivid. Pete felt like he was on one of those Saturday morning fishing shows on television.

"Walt, I thought you said that you knew all the spots."

"No, Pete, *you* said I knew all the spots. I think that this is going to be one of those days."

"Walt's right, Pete, we probably should start heading in so we can get you settled in your hotel."

"Hey, I'm getting a nibble here. What do I do?"

"Don't try to set it quite yet," Walt said. "Just bump it a bit. You'll know when he takes it."

The pole bent as if Pete had hooked an old boot. He jerked the rod back and the line ran out with a scream.

"Let it run or he'll break the line. Come up front by me," Walt said, scampering out of the way.

"Man, I can't believe how hard this thing is pulling."

"Gotta be a big ol' red. He's slowing down now. Start reeling him in. Be patient. This may take a few minutes. It's like sex, Pete. It's better if you don't rush it."

"I'll remember that, Walt. Darn, he's taking out all that line I just pulled in."

"Welcome to the Low Country," Clay said with a broad smile.

Pete worked the fish for five minutes until it tired and gave up the fight. Clay could not have planned it any better. Pete was already hooked better than the redfish.

"Watch your line, Pete. Don't let it rub the gunwale. Watch it; he's trying to go around the anchor line. Gimme that big net, Clay."

Walt slipped the net under a magnificent redfish and hoisted it into the boat. It flopped around on the deck for a few minutes and finally gave up.

"That thing's two feet if it's an inch," Clay said. "Hand me that measuring tape on the console. Man, I've seen beginner's luck before but this takes it. Twenty-six inches."

"Good job, Pete. Congratulations. Throw him on the ice in the bow storage compartment. Walt, why don't you pull up the anchor? We're going to get wet here in a few minutes."

In the excitement of the big catch, the three failed to notice the storm had moved above them. They raced through sprinkles back to the marina. A line of heavy showers followed one-half mile behind. The men quickly stored their gear and moored the skiff. Pete carried his trophy to the cleaning tables. From under cover, they watched the storm approach while Walt showed Pete how to clean a redfish. Lightning lit the dark late-afternoon sky, and thunder rumbled for miles. Rain, like Pete had never seen, poured from the heavens. The temperature dropped 10 degrees in five minutes.

"Walt, I don't know what I'm going to do with fresh fish in a hotel room. Why don't you take it home and eat it tonight."

"Thanks Pete, I think I will."

"How are you going to cook it?"

"That's easy. I lay out some tin foil and put the scale side down. Throw on some butter, Vidalia onions, and spices. Wrap it tight in the foil and put it on the grill on medium for 10 or 15 minutes. It melts in your mouth. You come over sometime and we'll have a feast."

Pete thought, wouldn't that be nice? He could fish on his days off and eat his catch with friends that night.

CHAPTER 10

▼

As a powerful member of the Appropriations Committee and a likely contender in the next presidential race, Buddy Duke enjoyed the adornments of power and influence. Usually he traveled with a small army of aids, interns, and other syco-phants who walked two steps behind, eager to satisfy every request and desire. This spring morning, however, he traveled from his home in Charleston unen-cumbered by his entourage. Buddy was vexed about the action that was being threatened against his long-time friend Dr. Wilhelm Betts. As he drove his wife's dark blue Cadillac Deville, he steamed about the butts he would need to kick in order to straighten things out. Soon to announce his run for the presidency, he didn't need this distraction.

As Duke strode toward the administrative offices at Hilton Head Hospital, all could see that he possessed the ingredients needed for success in politics. Women, especially young buxom political aids, found this rising star of the Democratic Party most appealing. This attractiveness translated not only into votes but also a few affairs. Voters liked his slim and tall physique, square jaw, and his full head of sandy blonde hair. His heavy cologne hung in the air after he passed through the foyer to meet Morton Bennett in the boardroom.

"Mort, I want to remind you how important Wilhelm is to me. When he saved my daughter from that damn brain cancer, he saved me, too. Lottie Ann means the world to me. I hate to think where I'd be now if she left us. You need to reassure me this problem is goin' away."

"Buddy, you need to relax about this."

Bennett once had Duke in his back pocket and now he was knuckling under like some green private. Buddy killed a potentially damaging investigation at Parris Island, allowing Bennett to retire without a mark on his record. There were allegations of improper use of funds and some rumors of embezzlement. After Buddy intervened, the problem vanished. Bennett figured that he should vanish also, so he took his retirement after 30 years in the Marines and moved to Hilton Head. Buddy figured Bennett still owed him.

"Every year when the medical staff elects a new president, this seems to come up in one form or another," Bennett said. "Fred Daniels is the new president. He wants to make his mark. We've always been able to show these doctors the right way to look at this. We'll get Daniels in step."

Duke walked behind Bennett to get a cold drink that he really didn't want. Years in Washington showed him that standing above and behind someone could be very intimidating.

"You had the last CEO tied around your little finger, as I remember."

"That's right," said Bennett.

Having been chairman of the hospital board of trustees for seven years, he held a firm grip on what happened at the hospital.

"Ol' Ray Watson was a good soldier. Did his duty without asking too many questions."

"What do you make of your new man?" asked Duke, still standing behind him leaning against the bar.

"Clay Stevens?" Bennett replied as he shifted in the high-backed oxblood leather chair. A plump man of 5 foot 7 inches, he looked a bit juvenile because his polished black wingtips barely touched the floor. With his jet-black hair slicked back and his pressed shirt and pants, he might have been waiting while his mother tried on a dress at Southfield's Department store in Charleston in 1947. "He's no lap dog, but I don't expect much trouble from him. He's nearing the end of his tour of duty with retirement in his sights. I don't see him stirring the pot too much."

Duke could see that he needed to remind Bennett of his obligation to him.

"I want you to be sure that Stevens backs off on this. Are you forgettin' Parris Island?"

"No, are you forgetting Da Nang?"

"Screw you, Mort. That was a lifetime ago." Buddy stepped into Bennett's view.

"And I figure we're all even now," Bennett barked as he stood to face Duke.

"Our lives are so intertwined by our screw-ups, being *even* is not on the damn radar screen. Listen, Mort, I didn't mean to snap at you. I need your help here. The only way I'll ever repay Betts for what he did for my family is to keep him happy and practicin' here on Hilton Head. It's in your own best interest anyway. You own a third of the damn lab."

"You're right. I'll put the pressure on Stevens to back off."

Pete chatted with the bell captain as Clay pulled his Jeep Cherokee up to the hotel entrance. The Westin reigned as the only five-star hotel on the island. Its prime mid-island beachfront location provided a stunning backdrop for its grand architecture. The hotel also proved to be an excellent recruiting tool for the hospital. The ocean view, room service, heated pool, and beachside bar worked magic. Pete lost his objectivity quickly. The job, the primary reason for the visit, fell second to *the life*—the island life of beach combing, sunbathing, and fishing. Never mind that he would be working 60 hours a week. *The life* was almost in his grasp.

"Good morning, Pete. You've got a big day ahead. Hope you rested well."

"I did, thanks. I woke up early and took a stroll on the beach. Awesome sunrise. I think that I've seen the sun rise from the ocean only once before."

"You're doing great. You need to be on your toes when you meet with the nurse manager, Joni Wheeler, and some of the medical staff. Even though the group that is leaving is terrible, they have been here long enough to make friends and allies. Everyone knows that I'm doing the right thing, but some have put up a fuss. Even though they complain constantly about the existing group, the nurses are nervous about getting to know a new set of doctors."

"Thanks for the advice. So, when do I get to meet your wife?"

"She died three years ago."

What an idiot, Pete thought. *How could I let out such a gaffe?* Pete needed to regain his focus and get through the interviews without stepping in a big pile of horse manure again. *Don't be an arrogant fool. I don't even have the job yet and I've decided to move already. Get it together.* "I'm sorry to hear that. I didn't mean to bring up a painful subject."

"That's OK. I'm at peace with it. We had a great marriage for 25 years. The kids were out of school and we had big plans. She went to her internist with belly pain one day. Did some blood work and ordered a CAT scan the next day. Pancreatic cancer. Mary was dead in three months. I'm glad she didn't suffer any longer. I've picked up the pieces now and life is good. It will never be the way it was, but I'm learning to live with it."

"Walt helped you, didn't he?"

"That he did. That he did."

Clay drove past the main entrance to the side of the hospital and ignored his reserved parking spot. With the heat of the day upon them, Pete began to sweat under his coat and tie. He tugged at his starched collar as they strolled past a small lagoon surrounded on three sides by pines. A 12-foot alligator sunned himself on the bank.

"There's a funny story about this lagoon and old Billy Joe here. When they dedicated this building, the founders thought it would be nice to rent some swans to have in the lagoon for the ceremony. Well, an hour before it started, the swans were nowhere to be found. There were plenty of feathers, though. The gator had swan sandwiches for lunch. The hospital had to buy the damn swans at $1,000 each. Billy Joe was given a reprieve by the hospital board. I'd a made boots out of him."

As they approached the administration entrance, Clay and Pete spotted Bennett and Duke who were talking outside the entrance. Bennett craned his neck in order to look Duke in the eye. To do otherwise, would entail a conversation with his shirt pocket.

"You see that short guy? That's Lieutenant Colonel Morton Bennett—chairman of the hospital board. You recognize the guy next to him?"

"Buddy Duke. I met him once at a social function in D.C.," Pete said, keeping with the plan to conceal their true relationship. He hadn't expected to see Buddy in person, which flustered him.

"He could be our next president," said Clay proudly as he fixed his tie and tucked in his shirt.

Clay made the introductions and Pete expressed his pleasure in meeting the distinguished men. "I'm sure you don't remember, but I met you at a United Way function in Washington."

"Do you live in the D.C. area, Peter?" Duke asked.

"Yes, Rockville," Pete said with a clandestine wink to Buddy.

"Beautiful area. Been there many times."

"Mort, Dr. Fredericks is a candidate for the head of emergency services," Clay interjected.

"Good for you, son," Bennett said coldly. "Clayton tells me he's got big plans for improvement there."

"So I hear," Pete replied. "I'm looking forward to taking a look around."

"We don't want to keep you gentleman, and I need to get Dr. Fredericks up to his interview," Clay said.

As they said their goodbyes, Pete could feel the sweat run down his back. He was never a very good liar so the charade with Buddy was making him nervous.

His mouth felt like he had been chewing dust. Clay escorted Pete up to the second floor to the emergency department. The ER had undergone two face-lifts since construction 15 years prior. The basic eight-room layout remained unchanged. The rooms fanned in a semicircle that faced a central nursing station. Everything shined. In Pete's experience, most ER's looked like small disaster areas. Usually carts and wheelchairs clogged the halls and counters, and desks were littered with stacks of paper and soda cans. Here, though, everything seemed to be in its place. Two large resuscitation rooms sat between three general-purpose treatment rooms on either side. Behind the nursing station hid two offices, a break room, and a sleep room for the doctors. The contrast between this bright and modern ER and the dungeon in Maryland opened Pete's eyes. He felt like a gangly teenager who grew two inches and filled out his physique over the summer. Now the pretty girls were interested in him.

"So, why put the ER on the second floor?" said Pete, a bit more comfortable back in his element.

"Hurricanes. All vital operations are above the first floor. I guess that's why I'm on the first floor.

Great question, smart guy. He wrestled with the idea of taking his coat off, knowing that this would expose the large wet area on his shirt from the sweat on his back.

"Joni Wheeler is a top-notch administrator. She's got a great group of nurses."

Joni Wheeler turned the corner from her office to find Pete and Clay standing in the middle of the ER. Clay made introductions and excused himself, promising to meet up with Pete for dinner.

"So what do you think of Hilton Head so far?" asked Joni as she tucked her long strawberry-blonde hair behind her ear.

"This is wonderful. I've had a fantastic time so far."

"Y'all must have gone fishing."

"That's right."

"None of the other candidates seem to enjoy the fishing. You must be the only one who fished before," she said in a sweet drawl.

"Clay asked me to keep quiet about it."

"Don't worry. Clay thinks we don't know about his little excursions with Walter. It's not what you might think. On those days when they fish, they'll both come back to the hospital and work 'til eight or nine at night or come in early the next day. Clay's a joy to work for."

"That's good to hear. Walt is a great guy, too."

"Oh, we love Walter. He is the heart and soul of this place. We were all crushed when his wife died. I could hardly face him for weeks after."

"Why is that?"

"One of our ER doctors sent his wife home when she was having a heart attack. By the time Walt brought her back, it was too late. We still feel terrible about it. Walter never held a grudge. He and I have talked about it. He says he loves us just the same as before. I think he's a saint."

"He didn't sue the doctor, did he?"

"You're right, Pete. You have good insight into people. I want to ask you what you plan to do with our current doctors if you're selected for the position."

"Clay gave me the impression that he wants to clean house. I plan to bring in all board certified doctors."

"Oh, I see," said Joni as she crossed her arms over her chest.

Wrong answer. Bzzzz. THANKS FOR PLAYING. Next contestant please. He hoped nobody was keeping track of his faux pas. Pete realized he should have tip-toed around that question. *There's one ally. What possible reason could she have to protect these guys? They're killing people off.* It didn't matter anyway. Pete figured that the entire day had been botched so far.

CHAPTER 11

▼

The gun fired. Pete bolted upright from a lounge chair on the porch of his hotel room. He knew it was a dream as soon as he opened his eyes. The dreams were less frequent now, but no less vivid. Sometimes he could smell the blood when he awakened. Pete fell back in the chair and waited for his heart rate to slow, but it jumped up again when the phone rang.

"I'm sorry to awaken you." It was Clay. "I want to make a change in the itinerary for tonight. Let's meet in your hotel lobby at 6:15. Dress casually."

"OK. I'll look for you then."

Pete's heart sank. This could only be bad news. He surmised that Clay wanted to make a quick rejection and avoid the discomfort of feigning interest during dinner. The ideas and plans that had circled in Pete's mind for the past several weeks vaporized. He was immediately transported back to Maryland. He could not imagine returning to the place that he had already abandoned emotionally. He showered, resigned to the fact that at worst he would be completely rejected and at best offered only a clinical position. He remembered Molly's advice about getting emotionally invested too soon. It seemed like good advice then, but turned out to be nearly impossible in practice. He put on his best game face for the meeting. Clay arrived early, dressed in clothing best kept for cleaning the garage.

"I'm sorry for the change in plans. Come sit by the pool."

As they moved through the large atrium lobby, Pete thought of Molly and all the good things that awaited him in Maryland. Even in her absence, Molly gave Pete comfort and strength.

"What a great night; too nice to be cooped up in a stuffy restaurant. I talked to everyone involved. You're the number one choice. So, what do you say? Come to Hilton Head to be my new ER director." Clay failed to tell him that he was the winner of a one-horse race.

"Clay, I'm flabbergasted. I've got to be honest with you. I was prepared to have you give me the heave ho right here. You've caught me completely off guard."

"Well, I'm honored then. I get the feeling that Dr. Peter Fredericks is not caught off guard very often."

"Of course I want the position. I'm thrilled. You know that I'll need to discuss this with my wife."

"Yes, of course. I want you to call Molly right now. I'd like her to come down while you're still here so she can see first hand. I don't want to rush you but I gotta get the wheels in motion."

Rush was an understatement. Clay needed Pete to get him out of an enormous jam. He was the last candidate, and time was running short to get people in place before the old group left. Forget about rushing. Run. Run down here, buy a house and get to work in the ER or there would be hell to pay with the board.

"Clay, thank you so much for putting faith in me."

"I know you're up to it, Pete. I'm going to sit by the beach for a few minutes. Call Molly on my cell phone right now. See if she can fly down here tomorrow. If it doesn't work out, we'll fly you both down later in the month."

Pete took a moment to clear his head. He had begun to organize a hypothetical presentation to Molly, but his self-doubt and surprise from Clay caused any collection of thoughts to scatter. He could tell Molly's surprise as they set plans.

"Well, what'd she say?" asked Clay as Pete approached him by the beach.

"She's thrilled and eager to come down. She's checking flights for tomorrow. Knowing Molly, we should expect her by noon and she'll have a house picked out by dinner."

"Great. Let's go see Walter. He's cooking up something good for us."

"Awesome. I'm starved. On our way there, I'd like to hear about Dr. Betts."

"You're going to be involved with this at some point, so I may as well fill you in now. You'll be on the executive committee and this is about to come up. Wilhelm Betts practices a unique brand of oncology. We don't have another cancer specialist on staff, so none of the physicians on the quality assurance committee knows if what he is doing is proper or not. They have kicked it up to the executive committee, which is a smart thing to do. There's no reason for any of them to stick their necks out."

"Quality Assurance is all confidential. Why should they feel that they are sticking their necks out?"

"QA is more complicated than that with Betts. He has big supporters on the medical staff, the board, plus Buddy Duke. Lots of cash involved. I don't know the whole picture but I'm doing some pokin' around. Don't get your shorts in a knot about it. You'll be an innocent bystander on the executive committee, so don't sweat it. If you haven't learned by now, though, I want you to understand something. If you threaten someone's cash flow, even if it's in QA, you'll become his enemy. You should always be very discreet about these matters—like a battle plan in war."

Pete thought about Dickman and whether he had done the right thing with his drunken partner. *Screw Dickman. I'm leaving anyway.*

"OK. That's enough business for tonight. Let's go see what ol' Walt's cooking for dinner."

CHAPTER 12

▼

Pete studied a map of the island at the entrance of the hotel as Rick Dawson arrived. Pete was happy that they were close in age, but he could see how Rick's boyish looks might make the retirees want someone older looking than a grandson. He lived up to his image of being a free spirit by wearing plaid Bermuda shorts, leather loafers with no socks, and a dark blue golf shirt. After introductions, they made the quick trip to the airport. Molly's plane departed late from Washington, so they had time to chat while sitting on a bench near baggage claim.

"So, how long have you lived here?" Pete asked.

"I moved from Columbia about three years ago. My wife and I parted ways before she could completely bankrupt me."

"High maintenance, huh?" Pete said, thankful that Molly could not be described that way.

"Tell me about it. I made good money as an accountant but she managed to spend it before the ink could dry on the back of the paycheck. I didn't really like accounting anyway. So here I am living in the best place doing something I like."

"Here's Molly now," Pete said as he ran to hug her. "How was your trip?"

"Boring until the last twenty minutes. That view coming down the coast is awesome."

"Yeah, I loved that, too," Pete said as he beamed with more excitement than Molly had seen in years. "Come meet Rick Dawson."

Pete, Molly, and Rick spent the day touring the plantations. Pete could tell from her reaction that the Hilton Head style of architecture did not please Molly.

Most of the homes had open floor plans, large angular windows, and stained-wood siding.

"This island is wonderful, Pete. I can't say that I'm thrilled about the housing options, though. I just think that I would be happier with a more traditional style home."

"But you like the idea of coming here?"

"Yes, if this job is what you want, I'm all for it. Find me a house that I can get excited about and I'll start packing."

After finishing with Rick, Pete and Molly headed to Walter's for dinner. Riding double on a rented moped, they cruised 278 to the north end. Molly rubbernecked at the lush landscape along the way. They found Walter at his pier, baiting his crab trap.

"This must be Miss Molly. I've heard wonderful things about you. It's a pleasure to meet you."

"The pleasure's all mine. From what I hear, you should get a recruiting fee for landing my husband."

"Well, I try to do my part. Pete's a good egg and he knows how to fish, too. You can never have enough fishin' buddies. Tell me what ya'll did today."

"Pete and I got the big tour from Rick and we went through a few places in Hilton Head Plantation," Molly said, as she peered into the crab trap and crinkled her nose. A foul-smelling chicken half sat at the bottom of the trap.

"Wha'dya think?" Walt said as he lowered the trap into the water.

"This type of architecture is new to me. I don't think that I like it, but maybe it needs to grow on me. I do like the style of the homes down here at this end." Molly turned to admire Walter's brick low country style house.

"Pete, did you know that Joni and Bill Wheeler are building not too far from here?" Walt said, as he pointed off to his right.

"She told me that she was building but didn't say where."

"Ya know the area 'cause we were there. If you want, we can walk down. It's about a quarter mile."

"Let's go," Molly said eagerly. I need to stretch my legs after all this riding in cars and planes today."

The three strolled along the dusty unpaved road that Walter had walked most of his life.

"I bet there's been some changes here over the years," Molly said.

"It all depends on where ya comin' from. We all take different roads to Hilton Head. For me, my life and my neighborhood aren't too much different than before all the development. I go to work, fish, and enjoy my family and friends the way I did 20 years ago."

"What do you think about all the communities with the gates and the guards?" asked Pete.

"It don't bother me. Folks have a right to live the way they please. I'm not sure what they need the gates for. I s'pose they want their privacy. Crime's never been a problem here. The last murder was five years ago when a retiree shot his wife and then killed himself."

"Did they know why he did it?" Molly said.

"They say he was depressed. He's probably one of those guys who flunked retirement."

"What do you mean?" Pete asked.

"Lots of folks come here expectin' that life will be better than it was in New York or Ohio or Pennsylvania. They work their whole lives to retire and come here thinkin' that whatever was makin' them sad up North will go away. They find out that their problems follow them." Walt paused to toss a fallen branch off the road. A pheasant scurried from the thicket. "Movin' to Hilton Head never cured alcoholism or fixed a bad marriage. If they had no hobbies and only worked at their job before, they become bored quickly. Most adapt right away to island life and really enjoy it. There's a few that never come around though. OK, this is the lot where the Wheelers are building. I guess you can't tell too much with just the framin' done."

"Oh, I can tell more than you'd think," Molly said as she stepped on to the lot.

Pete just kept his mouth shut. Walt was doing a much better job than he could ever do. Molly and Walt discussed the layout while Pete enjoyed the cool evening.

"Walt, is that your Aunt Verbena's house two lots over?" Pete chimed as the light bulb went off over his head.

"That's the one."

"Oh, Pete, it's wonderful," Molly said peering through the studs from the second floor.

"It's for sale by Walt's mom. She just inherited it. Do you want to check it out?"

"Let's go," Molly said, leading the way.

Molly seemed more excited than when they decided to buy the house in Rockville. It couldn't have worked any better if Walt and Pete had planned it. Pete didn't need a recruiter for Molly. He had Walt. Walt didn't need a real estate agent. He had Pete.

"I want to get the record straight from the start 'cause I don't want my buddy Dawson gettin' mad at me. Y'all asked to see the house and I'm just opening the door for you. Whatever happens after that is between you and my mama."

"OK, Walt. We get the picture. How old is the house?" Molly said, taking the front steps.

"Around a hundred years. You're gonna find the plumbing and the electric is all bad. This house needs lots of work and love. I hear that's your specialty."

"I think that I'm getting pretty good at fixing up old houses. I learned a lot doing our home in Maryland. This place is a diamond in the rough. It's good construction. The floors and the woodwork are in good shape. We could rip out the kitchen, extend it out the back, add a garage with a playroom above it, and do new plumbing and electric. In three months, we could move in and the whole thing could be finished in nine months. If you can work with me in your spare time, Walt, it will be done by Thanksgiving."

Molly spent the next hour inspecting, stepping off room sizes, and making sketches. Pete and Walter sat on the pier discussing fishing and life. Molly emerged with a broad smile and a gleam in her eye.

"This is it. An extra $100,000 will do it. It will be perfect when it's done. What do you say?"

Pete and Walt just looked at each other and smiled.

"Let's get together with Walt's mother tomorrow and work out a deal," Pete said.

The trio ate a fine meal of redfish and crab at Walter's, and enjoyed cold beer sitting in the back yard. Pete could tell from her expressions that Molly enjoyed Walter's tales of his life and times on the island. If this was what low country life offered, then Pete needed no more convincing.

On the way back to the hotel, they found their way down a dark dirt road and parked at the dunes. A full moon guided them to the beach. Not a soul could be seen or heard. Pete felt a chill from the mild ocean breeze and pulled Molly close. Waves lapped at the shore as they stopped and embraced. The breeze and the sound of the waves washed over Pete, cleansing him of his unsettled feelings. The tensions of the past few days and months washed to the depths of the sea. They held a tight embrace while standing on the sand. As they took turns removing pieces of clothing from each other, they caressed and kissed. Molly pulled Pete down onto the cool sand with her. They giggled like teenager lovers who had snuck down to the beach while they were supposed to be at the movies. Molly rubbed Pete's back as he lay face down on the clothes they spread out. This excited her as much as him. Pete turned to face her. He could see the moon and the stars reflect in her eyes as they made love with tenderness and with the excitement of finding a home on Hilton Head.

CHAPTER 13

▼

"It's tempting to hang up my political running shoes and live here with you on the beach," mused Buddy Duke as he and Wilhelm Betts sat on the patio overlooking Port Royal Sound and the Atlantic Ocean. Both enjoyed expensive French red wine as they took in the view. Duke always made Betts feel that the home belonged to Betts even though Duke truly owned the place. When Betts moved his practice to the island, Duke purchased the two million dollar estate with the understanding that his friend Wilhelm could live as his guest indefinitely. Even among the 10,000 square-foot homes of the Port Royal Plantation shoreline, the home stood out. The original builders modeled the home after an antebellum plantation home near Charleston. Impressive white pillars supported a two-level veranda that wrapped the home on three sides. Formal gardens surrounded the brick walkway that lead to a wooden bridge over the dunes. In the side yard, an elevated brick patio surrounded a kidney-shaped pool with a mosaic tile bottom.

"When you complete second term as president, you can do that," offered Betts. The large-framed, round-faced, doctor stood with his near empty glass and walked to retrieve the wine bottle from a large oval glass table. He filled both glasses, then slowly paced near the edge of the pool.

"You look uptight, Wilhelm. I told you everything will be fine. Bennett has things under control."

"I don't believe it. Bennett is telling what you want to hear," said Betts, with voice raised and face flushed. The unflappable and reserved Betts never acted this way. "I know this Daniels. Backing down from doing quality review he will not do." He set his glass on the table as his hands gently shook.

"Bennett told me that they've always been able to get the medical staff leadership to get in step with us. Come sit down. You're gettin' all fired up for nothin'. Tell me why this gent is any different from the others."

"The others are rich from me. The last president—a general surgeon. Two or three good operative cases a week, I gave him. The one before him—an anesthesiologist. They're on the gravy trail. Daniels is a goddamn eye doctor. I don't send him cases. Nothing, he has to lose."

He has plenty to lose, Duke thought. But he wanted to try the carrot before using the stick. If they could find a way to get him on the gravy train, life would be easier for everyone. Surely some type of monthly stipend could be arranged.

"What about Stevens? Bennett says he won't stir the pot."

Betts stood again, throwing his thick arms in the air. "Don't *listen* to Bennett. He's blowing smoke in your ear." Oblivious to his mixed metaphor, he began to pace again. "The likes of Stevens I have seen. He comes up like nice southern gentleman, but he'll screw me when he gets chance. He told me medical staff was doing quality review and he was not standing on the way." His pacing quickened as he downed his glass of wine.

"I hate to see you fret like this. Let's get some sleep. Things will look brighter in the mornin'," Buddy said.

"No, you go in. I sit her for a while and think."

As Buddy drifted inside, Betts dialed up Gibby Morgan. Gibby, Hilton Head's sheriff, had managed to position himself on the good side of every important person he encountered. Being an adept politician got him much further than being a good sheriff. Anyway, being sheriff of Hilton Head was not much of a challenge and did not require much crime-fighting skill. It was sort of like being the sheriff of Disney World. Dealing with the well heeled of Hilton Head for a decade, Gibby had honed his political skills nicely. A complimentary special duty officer here and a forgiven DUI offense there had won him many allies.

"Gibby, I have job that requires your unique skills."

Betts leaned forward in his chair and set his plans in place. Things would not look brighter in the morning and the time for action had come. He couldn't trust that Bennett would look out for his interests.

CHAPTER 14

▼

At 7 a.m., Pete's responsibilities for the ER at Hilton Head Hospital began. Months of preparation and anticipation lead to this moment. Feelings reminiscent of Christmas made him eager to open the package and see what was inside. He felt almost giddy walking through the main door to the ER. Nightshift nurses conversed with dayshift nurses at the desk as he approached. Southern hospitality lived. They all introduced themselves and showed Pete where to put his things. There were no patients in the department, so the conversation with the physician who was coming off duty was brief. Pete felt bad for the guy but felt no responsibility for his fate. He didn't create the problem; he had come to fix it. His face beamed. Although he felt some anxiety about adjusting to his new work environment and fitting in with the medical staff, his enthusiasm for the challenge ahead of him overshadowed any apprehension.

Clay soon arrived with his Chief Financial Officer, Larry Carver. An overweight, pale, balding man who appeared to be 10 years older than his age of 60, Carver was the epitome of the corporate clock puncher, doing his mundane job every day and hoping to maintain the status quo. Clay held Carver in low regard but had no immediate plans to get rid of him. There were too many other fish to fry. They found Pete talking with Victoria Jackson. Clay admired Vickie's curvaceous figure and short, stylish brown hair as they approached. A few crows' feet accented her kind brown eyes.

Clay smiled and winked at Victoria while no one was looking. "Larry has been with the hospital for about seven years now and does a great job for us. He also serves as the financial officer for the Hilton Head Hospital Foundation."

"Wonderful. I didn't realize that a foundation exists. How much is in it, Larry?"

"About 10 million dollars, Doctor. We've had some large donations recently," Carver said dully. We've done well in the market the past few years. Most people don't know too much about the foundation. We have a small board. Most of the members…"

"I'm sorry to interrupt," said Victoria, "I've got a man in a lot of pain."

Victoria Jackson waited for Pete as he approached. Little could shake this seasoned ER nurse. Although tough, she maintained empathy for the patients, and the consulting physicians liked her.

"This 30-year-old guy is beside himself. He says that he just woke up with severe pain in his ear. He's about ready to jump out of his skin."

"Let's go see him." Pete stepped quickly with Victoria a step behind. "Good morning, sir, I'm Dr. Fredericks. This is Victoria. I hear you're having some problems with your ear."

"I don't know what this is, doc. It's driving me crazy. This hurt so bad when I woke up, I made my wife bring me here right away."

Pete examined the tubby man's unaffected ear first and found a normal canal and eardrum. Sitting in the other canal was a large bug. The light made it move deeper into the canal.

"Ouch. Damn, there it goes again. I don't think I can take this much more."

"It's a cockroach. It must have crawled in your ear during the night. Did you sleep on the floor?"

"Sort of. Last night was our turn to sleep on the inflatable mattress on the floor."

"The cockroaches love it when people sleep on the floor. It's actually the most common bug removed from the ear, not that you probably care now. Give me a minute and we'll have it out. Why don't you lay down with the bug ear facing up?"

Pete could tell from the 'I told you so' glance the man shot at his wife that sleeping on the floor had been a bone of contention the previous night. Pete withdrew five cc's of a local anesthetic into a syringe and dripped it into the ear canal. Within a minute the insect was dead. As Pete peered into the ear, he gently grasped the insect with a long forceps and removed it, taking great care to avoid touching the delicate ear canal.

"This is quite a specimen. Vickie, have you had breakfast yet?"

"No thanks, I'll save it for later.

"Thanks, doc. I'll never forget this."

"You might want to call the rental agency and have 'em spray. Enjoy the rest of your time on the island. We'll have you on your way in just a few minutes."

"Palmetto bug," Vickie said smugly.

"Pardon me."

"It's a palmetto bug, not a cockroach, Pete."

"Looked like a roach to me."

"Look, if you're gonna be an islander, you're gonna have to learn the names of the local varmints. Palmetto bug is a much more pleasant name. Don't you agree?"

"Anything you say. Just lead me to the next patient."

"This is a 50-year-old man who has a fish hook in the back of his head."

They greeted a heavy-set, stoic man who was sitting comfortably on the exam stretcher.

"Hi, sir, I'm Dr. Fredericks. This is Victoria. Man, you really caught a whopper."

"You're telling me."

"How'd this happen?" Pete asked.

"My buddy got me on his backswing when he was casting. He and I tried to get it out but there was no way. The worst part is that we were catching fish left and right."

"Oh, yeah? Where were you?"

"I'll tell you but you can't broadcast it all over the island."

"Cross my heart," Pete said while motioning with his hands.

"This time of year, you can't miss if you go to the third inlet in from the south end. Wait until the tide is moving out. They practically jump in the boat."

"He's right. I've caught some fish there before," offered Vickie with a smile and a nod.

"You like to fish, huh?"

"Don't say it like a woman has never fished before, Dr. Fredericks."

Pete smiled, realizing that Vickie had spunk. Most nurses would wait a while to get to know a doctor before entering into the banter that was common between emergency physicians and nurses. This joking around released the tension of the ER, so Pete was happy to join the game.

"OK, Vickie. You and I can talk about fish later. Let's get this hook out of your head, sir. I need a minor tray and a sterile wire cutter."

"It's right behind you."

"Hey, you think of everything."

"I didn't just fall off the turnip truck, you know."

Pete donned his size 7 1/2 sterile gloves and prepared the skin of the balding man with iodine solution. From a short glass bottle, he withdrew Bupivicaine, a long-acting local anesthetic, into a syringe. He slowly infiltrated the skin around the hook using a small-gauge needle. Pete grasped the hook with a forceps and pushed the tip of the imbedded hook all the way through the skin so that the barb protruded. Using the wire cutters, he clipped the barb. The loose piece fired across the room and pinged along the floor. He then removed the hook, minus the barb, which had previously snared the skin. Direct pressure controlled the bleeding and Vickie applied a sterile dressing. After updating the patient's tetanus vaccine, she discharged the patient.

"So, how long have you been fishing?"

"Since I was three. My dad was a big fisherman. He used to enter tournaments and win prizes. It was like a religion at my house. I hardly ever go anymore, though. Have you been yet?"

"I've been with Walt and Clay Stevens a couple of times. You should come some time."

"I don't know. Let me think about it."

"All right. You let me know. I'm heading down to talk to Clay for a few minutes."

Clay sat at his desk reading the Wall Street Journal as Pete arrived. Between articles, he had been pondering how to present his idea to Pete. Clay needed the right person to serve on the foundation board, but knew that it was no prize for a doctor to serve. Most of the medical staff had shunned involvement with the board in the past. It was a boring position and few liked Tami Bennett, chairman of the board of trustees. She was difficult at best and at worst could be a terror. As Mort's sister, she used her relationship with him as a club. A few years prior, she divorced her plastic surgeon husband and reclaimed her maiden name. Tami had enough plastic surgery for the whole south end of the island. Because of all her cosmetic enhancements, she had become a bit scary looking. Her face appeared stretched and her breasts pointed in the same direction regardless of her position. Tami and her brother ran the board and the foundation like their own fiefdom. The board had always provided a rubber stamp in the past. Whatever Morton Bennett requested, the foundation obliged.

"I want to talk to you about the foundation. A long-time trustee has been in failing health and is goin' to resign. I want to nominate you to take her place. Your experience on the community foundation in Maryland would be very valuable."

"What would be involved if I decide to serve?"

"They meet every other month. It's usually a two-hour meeting held right here at the hospital. They occasionally have an ad hoc committee you might serve on. They've been doin' things pretty much the same way for the past 15 years. Most of the trustees have been on the board for more than 10 years. I need you to bring in a fresh perspective—you know, stir things up a bit. Rock the boat—just don't sink it. So what do you say?"

"Anything for you." *What's the harm?*

CHAPTER 15

▼

With his windows down, Clay drove to the estate of Lieutenant Colonel Morton Bennett. The cool breeze relaxed him while he considered his presentation about the latest Executive Committee meeting. The Bennett estate stood on wooded land overlooking the Intracoastal Waterway in Sea Pines Plantation. One of the few homes in the neighborhood that did not blend well with its surroundings, the massive home seemed large even for its four-acre lot. Bennett purchased the old plantation house from one of the original developers who had restored it from a dilapidated state. Tami Bennett, permanent guest of her brother, met him at the door. She was an attractive woman in her day but now was aging without grace. Tami maintained a good figure but her skin looked like leather and her blonde hair had a cheap metallic look. She wore a skimpy outfit that revealed her ample cleavage. She would fit right in at a casino in Vegas.

"Hello, Tami. How have you been?"

"Good evening, Clayton. I'm just fine. Mort is in his study. Go on in. Oh, by the way, Dr. Fredericks is now a foundation trustee. Will you tell him that I will call him soon?"

"That's great; I'll do that."

Clay made the familiar walk down the center hallway to the study. From his desk, Morton Bennett viewed a wide expanse of the waterway. He sat in his large leather chair reading a magazine.

"Have a seat, Clayton. What news do you have for me?"

"Most of the meeting was routine business, so I won't bore you. On the matter of Dr. Betts, we devised what I feel is a fair plan to review his method of practice."

"I'm all ears," Bennett said tersely, as he put his magazine aside.

Clay explained the plan, trying to put it in the best light. Three outside oncologists would review a sample of cases from Betts and make a pronouncement about the appropriateness of his practice. As Clay spoke, the furrows on the colonel's brow grew deeper. Clay wondered if steam would soon shoot from his ears. As Clay finished, Bennett rose to his feet.

"Goddamn it. I expected that you would steer this matter to a quiet resolution within our own doors. Now you've opened up Pandora's goddamn box, for Christ's sake. Is he really doing anything all that bad? Look at the people he has saved. Do I need to remind you of Senator Duke's daughter? Most of these people are almost dead when they get here. What's the harm in letting him take a crack at saving them?"

"You know this is a medical staff issue," Clay said, trying to pacify him. "There is unanimous support on the committee. This will be a fair inquiry. Fred Daniels is an honorable person. He's not leading some lynch mob here."

"We'll see about that. What else do you have?"

"We need to look into the arrangement between the hospital and Betts' lab."

"What about it?"

"Did you know we subsidize the lab by 40 percent?"

"Hell, yes. And I also know that he earns us a net one million every year. So what if we lose a little on the lab?"

"It may be illegal, Mort."

"Screw that. My lawyers reviewed this up and down. It's legal."

"What about the legislation in congress?"

"Screw those dimwits. There's plenty of opposition from the AMA and others. It will never make it through the Senate anyway. All right, so the damn cannon has been fired. Let's deal with what we can control now. We need to start swaying key members of the medical staff to our side."

"Mort, I'm not taking sides here. I've gone out of my way to be unbiased, so I'm not going to turn right around and do the opposite."

Bennett stood gazing at the waterway and took a drink of scotch.

"Listen, Clayton. I'm going to lay it out for you plain and simple. You're either with me or you're not on this. This island and this hospital have huge support from some very influential people in this state. They will not be happy if we mess with Betts. Trust me on this. You do not want to cross these people. What happens here could affect the entire island."

"You have my loyalty and respect but I'm going to remain neutral on this. It is essential for me to maintain credibility with the medical staff. We need to let this inquiry go forward. It's possible he'll get a mixed or neutral review and we can put it behind us. You make strong arguments, but this is in the hands of the medical staff now."

"Damn that Daniels. None of this would have happened if he had looked the other way like the others. All right. You keep me posted on this. I don't want any surprises. Got it?"

Clay drove by Walter's house to find him sitting comfortably in a chair by a fire in the back yard.

"You got a beer for your old buddy?"

"Do bears crap in the woods? Have a seat. What do you know?"

Clay cracked open a cold beer from Walt's omnipresent cooler and settled into an Adirondack chair. Twilight had surrendered to the night. Only an occasional pop and crackle from the fire could be heard.

"The Little General just chewed my ass about this mess with Betts. I told him about our plan to review the way Betts practices and he blew a gasket."

"So what are you going to do?"

"We're moving ahead. I'm not going to let Bennett and the Silicone Princess run the show at this hospital. He'll see he's overstepped his bounds and will back off after a few days of pissing about it."

"You sound upset. I guess the honeymoon is over, huh?"

"The more I think about it, the more it gets under my skin. Why should he think he can muscle his way into a quality issue? I've seen this type of behavior before, but never from a board chairman."

"I reckon that when you can't explain somebody's behavior; just follow the money. That usually gives you the answer."

"I don't know, Walt. Bennett is a rich man. I doubt pay-offs from somebody would influence him. I'm not going to get an ulcer about it."

"That's good. Have another beer. Anyway, what's the worst they could do to you?"

"Fire me."

"Are you prepared to go to the wall on this?"

"Hell, yes. I've conducted myself in an honest fashion all my life. I'm not bending over for Bennett. I'm not afraid of being pushed out. I've got enough put away that I can live comfortably off the interest. I call it my screw-you money."

"Screw-you money, huh?"

"Yeah. I don't need to have this job and I don't need to take crap from the likes of the Little General. I enjoy what I do but if comes down to it, I won't mind saying 'screw you' and walking away. Enough about this. When are we goin' fishin' next?"

CHAPTER 16

▼

After several days off, Pete eagerly returned to work to find an empty emergency department at 7 a.m. Victoria sat drinking a cup of coffee on a bench outside the ER.

"Did you have a nice time when you were off?"

"Sure did. Batteries are recharged and I'm ready to work. So, how long have you known Clay?" A big smile spread across Pete's face.

"Just a few months. What are you getting at?"

"I see the way you two look at each other."

"Was it that obvious?"

"It must be 'cause I'm usually the last person to notice these things."

"Can I tell you something in confidence?" Victoria said, blushing.

"Yes, by all means."

Vickie went on to detail her romance with Clay. Since her divorce, she dated little but this changed quickly after meeting Clay. Over several months, they grew very close. They enjoyed their private time together, trying to keep it quiet around the hospital.

"Can you keep this under your hat? The last thing I need to deal with is a lot of workplace gossip. I really didn't intend for this to happen, but I'm glad it did. The whole thing was very spontaneous."

"I'm very happy for you and yes, I can keep a secret." *Boy can I keep a secret.*

The clerk stuck her head out of the ER door. "Dr. Fredericks. Victoria. Cardiac arrest. Five minutes out."

"Let's get to work," Pete said, eager for some action.

Pete and Vickie were preparing the resuscitation room as EMS arrived.

"Doc, this is a 16-year-old male. His mom couldn't awaken him this morning," said the paramedic, shaking his head side to side. One paramedic compressed the chest up and down while another breathed for the patient with a ventilation apparatus. "Monitor showed a rate of 40 but we couldn't get a pulse. He's had two rounds of epinephrine and atropine. He's got good breath sounds after we tubed him."

"OK, fellas," Pete said, feeling less enthused for the action. Let's move him over here. Man he's cold."

With one swift motion, they moved the sandy-haired young man on the spine board over to the ER stretcher. There was no pulse. They put him on the heart monitor and continued CPR.

"Let's give him one mg of epi and get a warming blanket. Keep that CPR going. Good strong rapid compressions."

The paramedic handed Pete a plastic camera-film container. Something rattled inside it. "We found it next to his bed."

Pete opened it and dumped a familiar-looking pale green pill onto his palm. OC on one side and 80 on the other. "This is OxyContin. Did you give him Narcan to reverse it?"

"No. I've never seen that kind of pill before," the paramedic said nervously.

"Don't worry. I don't know many pills on sight, but I know this one," Pete said. "Vickie, give him two mg of Narcan and another dose of epinephrine."

Vickie gave the medication through the IV, but there was no improvement. "Pete, you're not gonna like the rectal temp I got—89."

"Man, he's been dead for a while. Was he under the covers in bed when you found him?" Pete quizzed the paramedic.

"Yeah, and his room was warm."

"Shit. He's dead. Stop CPR," Pete said dejectedly.

As Vickie shut off the monitor, the room became church quiet. Vickie and several technicians stood at the bedside while tears flowed from their eyes. Feeling defeated, Pete stood motionless with his head bowed. Joni Wheeler broke the silence when she walked in the room.

"Oh, dear God. This is Billy Rivers. Oh, Lord. My Bill is going to be crushed by this."

"How did you know him, Joni?" Vickie said, drying tears.

"My husband has been like a father to this boy. His mother used to work for Bill. She had Billy out of wedlock and never married. He and Bill have been very close."

"I'm so sorry, Joni. There was nothing we could do. I think he died of an OxyContin overdose," Pete said.

"My God. I can't believe that scourge has made it to Beaufort County," Joni said, as she ran her hands through Billy's sandy hair.

"I need you to come with me to talk to his mother," Pete said.

Pete had seen many people die, most of them old. Many were ancient nursing-home patients who waited for death to come. It was usually easy to speak to families and go on with the day. It would not be so easy speaking to the mother of a boy who was waiting for life to come.

Pete walked by the nursing station on the way back from the lobby, glancing at the charts of a 4-year-old with a fever and a 75-year-old with gout in the big toe. He motioned for Victoria to follow him into the call room. As Pete sat across the bed, he offered the easy chair to Victoria.

"Are you OK?"

"I'm not sure, Vickie. I don't want to just plow back into seeing patients without sitting down for a minute to talk about this. Those two out there can wait. How are you?"

"I'm sad," Vickie said. "I feel so bad for his mother. I'd probably feel worse if I had kids of my own."

"Yeah, I know. This really sucks. Now this lady is all alone. Can you think of anything else we could have done?"

"No. You're right. He was probably dead for a while."

"You did a wonderful job, as always. You're an excellent nurse. Thank you for being here with me. You know, we need to take time to remind each other how hard our job is sometimes. I want you to know that I appreciate your hard work. I'm trying to not let shit like this take a bite out of me. I want to be stronger because of this; not weak or cynical."

"Can I ask you something?" Victoria said, leaning forward in her chair.

"Anything."

"Were you praying after you pronounced him dead?"

"No. Just collecting myself."

"Are you very religious?"

"Not really. My parents pretty much rammed it down my throat when I was growing up. By the time I got to college, I had enough of it."

"Clay and I have talked about God a few times so I've been thinking about it lately. I haven't let many people into my life since my divorce. I certainly haven't let God in. It's not something I've tried to do on purpose; I just haven't been with Him. You know what I mean?"

"Sure, I can relate to that."

The clerk interrupted with a call from the desk.

"Sheriff Morgan is here to see you."

"OK, I'll be right out."

"We better get back to it, Pete."

"Take your time. Collect yourself while I talk to the sheriff."

Pete found four charts waiting as he passed by.

"What do you know, doc?" Gibby said as he lumbered up to Pete.

"Couldn't save him. I think it was OxyContin. I guess the autopsy will show it. You been seeing much trouble with that stuff."

"Yeah. Last few months, it showed up in a couple of busts in Beaufort."

Little other work could be done while caring for Billy Rivers, causing the ER to be mired in chaos. Thankfully, the police left, and the body was on the way to the coroner. The trauma room looked like a bomb went off. Discarded medical supplies littered the floor and counters. Angry patients cluttered the lobby. Pete could never understand how somebody with a cut finger would complain about waiting while he cared for a heart attack or gunshot wound. People could be such assholes. He and the nurses often joked about needing to put in a drive-through window.

The day seemed to go on forever. Near the end of his shift, Pete picked up the chart of Roger Bond, a 20-year-old patient who was vacationing from Ohio. Upon reviewing the chart, Pete found normal vital signs and a chief complaint of "Paranoid."

"Hello, I'm Dr. Fredericks. I apologize for your wait. How can I help you this evening?"

"Are you with the bureau?" Roger said, with a strange look in his eyes.

"Excuse me?"

"Are you with the FBI?" Roger said, quickly shifting his tall frame on the cart.

"No, Roger, I am not. I'm here to help you. Why are you concerned about the FBI?"

"They've been following us since we left Ohio. They're everywhere—the beach, the condo. They tap our phone; listen to us with supersonic microphones; watch us from satellites. I can even hear them talk on the radio."

"You hear them in your head?"

"Yeah, could hear them talking when I was waiting."

"Do you hear any other voices?"

"I can hear the IRS talk to the FBI. They're gonna put me in jail 'cause I didn't pay taxes."

"So what are you going to do now?"

"We came to get on a sailboat to take us to Bermuda. No FBI in Bermuda. Safe in Bermuda. I gotta go. Gonna find me."

"Slow down now. Where is your family?"

"Mom's at the condo. Dad said we had to stop here for tests before we get on the boat. Gotta go, man. Bermuda, man. I can hear 'em."

As Pete and Roger spoke, Roger's father returned from a quick trip to the vending machines. His face bore the worry over Roger's problems.

"Take it easy, son. Everything will be fine. Hi doc, I'm Robert Bond. May I talk to you out here for a minute? Son, we'll be right back."

"Tell me, what's going on with Roger?"

"Doc, I'm afraid we've made a big mistake bringing Roger to the island. We hoped the trip here would help him, but it seems to have made things worse."

"What was happening that made you feel a trip here would help him?"

"Roger used to be a bright student. He was not himself over this break from Miami University. He was withdrawn all Christmas break and didn't want to spend time with his friends. He had been back to school for several weeks when we learned that he wasn't attending any of his classes. His dorm supervisor called us to suggest that he withdraw from classes for a semester. Now he says strange things and talks about the FBI, the IRS, and wiretaps. I thought that maybe it was just stress, so we came down from Ohio to our condo—thinking we could work it out. We're in over our heads now and we don't know what to do."

"You are wise to bring him in. He needs to be hospitalized in our psychiatric unit to sort this out. He's at great risk for flight because of his paranoid thoughts. Normally, I would have a deputy stand by, but seeing someone in uniform is likely to make things worse. I'm going to examine him and draw some blood. You'll need to stay with him so that he doesn't slip out. I'll be completing paperwork to commit him to the hospital for a few days until the psychiatrist can do a full assessment and make final recommendations."

"What is doing this to him? I can't stand to watch this, doc. Is it drugs?"

"We are going to do a drug screen, but I doubt that's the answer. The psychiatrist will need to give a final diagnosis, but I am concerned Roger has schizophrenia. That's most likely why he is paranoid and acting so strangely."

Pete performed a physical, neurological, and psychological exam. After being assured that nothing would be injected into him when they drew blood, Roger agreed to have blood drawn and to give a urine sample. As Pete prepared to see another patient, a deputy who was investigating an auto accident walked through the ER. The deputy stopped at the desk in full view of Roger and his paranoid delusions. Roger bolted past his father, bowling Pete over as he made his way out of the room. Roger plowed into the deputy, causing both to tumble to the ground. The deputy's head sounded like a melon falling off the fruit stand when it hit the floor. Jack Gurba lay unconscious as blood flowed from the back of his head. Unharmed in the collision, Roger released Gurba's gun from its holster. All eyes turned to the scrambling schizophrenic as he made his way to the door. Pete collected himself while he moved to help Deputy Gurba.

"Call 911. Tell them we have an officer down and a—a—a patient with a gun. Tell the dispatcher to tell the responding deputy to call me on Gurba's radio." Pete was searching for a good word to describe Roger but all he could think of was crazy. He didn't want Roger's father to hear his son called crazy across a crowded ER.

As Roger left the ER, he saw flashers approaching. His delusional state did not allow him to consider that this was an ambulance. As the ambulance reached the bottom of the ramp, Roger fired once, disabling the upper flasher panel.

A nurse took the radio call from a distressed paramedic.

"Hilton Head Hospital. This is EMS 5. What the hell is going on up there? Somebody just shot our lights out. We've got a 50-year-old man with chest pain. What do you want us to do?"

"Dr. Fredericks. Did you hear that radio transmission?"

"Yes, Catherine. Tell them to put on two liters of oxygen, an inch of nitro-paste, start an IV, and back up out of view with lights off and wait until we tell them to proceed. Somebody get a collar to immobilize Gurba's neck and put a pressure dressing on his head. Call out the CAT scan tech and tell her to come in the front of the hospital. X-ray his neck while he's over there. Somebody else help me get Gurba's bullet-proof vest off."

Roger looked like a caged animal as he stood near the vending machines at the top of the ramp that came up the back side of the hospital to the ER. All he could do was pace and be agitated. "Don't you IRS assholes come any closer. I'm gonna shoot you again."

Having immobilized Gurba's neck, the nurses removed his vest and placed him on a backboard. Pete removed his lab coat, donned the protective vest, and buttoned his lab coat over it.

"Hilton Head ER. This is Deputy Lacy. Come in."

Pete searched for Gurba's radio beneath the blanket covering him.

"This is Dr. Fredericks. Go ahead Lacy."

"Tell me what's happening, doc. How is Gurba?"

"We've got a real bad deal here. Gurba is unconscious. A crazy man has his gun and has already fired at an ambulance. Right now he is on the ramp near the ER doors. He is agitated and very paranoid. Don't let him hear your sirens or see your lights. It will just make him worse."

Crazy. There. He said it. There was no time and no need to explain the paranoid delusions associated with schizophrenia. This guy was truly crazy. Not a little neurotic or depressed. He and reality parted ways a while back and nearly anything could happen.

"Doc, I'll be there in five minutes. It'll be 10 more until I have good back up."

"OK. I'm gonna occupy him until you can figure a way out of this. I've got Gurba's vest on."

"Doc, don't even think about getting into this guy's sight. Let me worry about that."

"All right. Just don't shoot him unless you have to. This guy is not a criminal. He's just sick."

Pete walked to the automatic door, staying out of Roger's sight. As he approached the door, the sensor tripped and the door opened. Pete could hear Roger talking nonsense to himself. He had no experience with this type of situation. There was no lecture in residency on what to do with a psychotic who was waving a handgun. He did know that someone had to talk to Roger before his paranoid delusions got him into more trouble.

"I ain't goin' to jail," stammered Roger.

"Roger. It's Dr. Fredericks. I want to help you."

"Damn noise—stop the goddamn noise," Roger yelled as he paced.

"I just want to help you, Roger. Did the truck at the bottom of the ramp pull away?"

"Yeah."

"There you go, Roger. It's quiet now. Nobody wants to hurt you. They're leaving you alone."

"How 'bout that agent inside? IRS bullets."

"Don't worry about him. He won't bother you. Can I get you something?"

"FBI, IRS, Coca-Cola."

"Sure, Roger. How about a Coke? I'll toss you 50 cents to use in the machine."

"Fifty cents. Mom's got 50 cents for Juicy Fruit."

"I want you to have something to drink, Roger. You promise not to shoot at me if I come out alone?"

"Yeah, come on out."

As if on guard duty in some nutty cartoon, Roger paced with long strides, swinging his gun at his side and looking in all directions. Soaked with perspiration, his brown hair lay matted against his gaunt face. Pete stepped slowly into Roger's view. He tossed one quarter at a time to Roger who used them to buy a cold can of Coke.

"Why don't we sit and talk for a while, Roger?"

"Talk. Talk about Juicy Fruit—go ahead."

"I'm tired, Roger. I'm going to sit on the curb here. I figure if we both sit and talk, we might come up with a way out of this mess. What do you say?"

"OK, doc."

Roger sat with his knees up to his chest, shifting the gun between hands as he looked down the ramp. Pete sat cross-legged, catty-corner from Roger.

"You do much fishing, Roger?"

"Dad and me used to go. Never caught much."

"Did you enjoy it?"

"Yeah. I guess."

"Tell me about it."

"We had a boat. Took it on Lake Erie before the government stole it. We would try to catch perch and walleye. Waaaaal eyyyyyes. That's like eyes in the back of your head, man. Those FBI agents have that, ya know. They see everything. They can hear us talking now. I hear *them* talking now."

Pete and Roger's little trip to reality was brief. Roger returned to his tirade on the FBI and the IRS. As Roger became more agitated and delusional, Pete saw a figure in the dark who was making his way up the ramp behind the parked cars. Roger stood again and began to pace. Deputy Lacy crouched behind a sedan across from Pete, providing a clean shot at Roger.

"They're coming. I'll off myself. IRS, FBI gonna kill me anyway."

The vest was making Pete hot already. Flashbacks to Billy Flick zoomed in and out. His heart raced and bouts of nausea and dizziness came like waves on the shore.

Roger raised his gun pointing it at his own chin, leaving Deputy Lacy no choice. Lacy fired, hitting Roger in the right forearm. Roger dropped the gun and fell to the ground screaming in pain.

"I toooold you. Dad, where's dad? Dad, Dad, help."

Lacy retrieved the gun while Pete went to get help. Pete and a nurse returned with a stretcher and leather restraints. Still agitated, Roger was wrestled to the stretcher, restrained, and given a shot of Thorazine.

Gibby Morgan arrived as they wheeled Roger inside.

"Hey, doc. You OK here?

"Hey, Gibby. I don't know if it's you or me, but one of us is bad luck. We gotta stop having these little meetings," Pete said, shaking his head. "I think things are about under control now. Gurba is in CAT scan now. They tell me he is awake. He probably just got his bell rung. We'll see what the scan shows."

"Doc, I know you're busy, but I have to take your statement sometime tonight."

CHAPTER 17

▼

At the end of the shift, a reporter waited outside for Pete. Knowing the story would be sensationalized, Pete took the back stairs down from the ER, hoping to avoid another interview about a sad story. He met Walter on the stairs.

"Hey, Walt, how have you been?"

"Can't complain," Walter said, out of breath.

"You don't look well. Are you OK?"

"To tell you the truth, I've been feeling tired since lunch. I started having some pain in my chest about an hour ago."

"And you were just going to keep this to yourself? Come on. You're coming with me to the ER right now."

"Pete, I'll be OK. Just lemme get home and rest. I'll be fine in the morning. I've had this chest pain before."

"What's the longest before today?"

"Ten minutes—probably."

"Has it been constant for the past hour?"

"Yeah, I guess."

"Walt, you've been having angina before and now you're probably having a heart attack. I'm not going to argue with you about this. You're my good friend and I'm not letting you go home without getting checked out first. Let's go."

Pete and Walt walked slowly back to the ER. Pete escorted him to a bed and motioned for the nurses to set the wheels in motion for a cardiac work up. While the EKG was being done, Pete briefed his new partner, Gabe Paulson, on Walter's story. Gabe had just relieved Pete at the end of his shift. Pete also reminded Gabe of what had happened to Walt's wife.

The tech dropped the EKG in front of Pete. It showed a heart attack in the front of the heart. Pete dialed as he read the EKG.

"Clay, this is Pete. I'm sorry to bother you."

"That's OK. I was just going to call you. Vickie told me about the shooting. I was off the island all day today."

"It's not about the shooting. Walter is having a heart attack. We've got the cardiologist on the way now to take him to the cath lab. I thought that you would want to be with him."

"Thanks, Pete. I'm on my way. I'll call his family."

Pete found Walt sweating and out of breath. Walt winced and gripped the railing of the cart. Pete had seen this expression many times on cardiac patients. Gabe Paulson had things well in hand but Pete was still concerned. Glad that Gabe was there to manage the situation, he pulled up a chair and held Walt's hand. Pete knew the danger and that time was all important—even more important with his good friend beside him on the stretcher.

"I don't want to scare you, but you're having a heart attack. Clint Cato is on his way to see you. They need to take you to the heart cath lab to get your artery open."

"Whatever it takes, Pete. Thanks, buddy."

"It was just dumb luck that I came across you on the stairs. Any other day…"

"Not luck at all," Walt said with a weak smile. "Thanks for being here with me."

"Wouldn't be anywhere else."

Walter drifted off. Pete could smell urine and realized that Walter had wet himself. The monitor toned loudly. Gabe and the nurses responded immediately. The monitor showed ventricular tachycardia, a deadly heart rhythm seen commonly in heart attack patients. The nurses applied two conductive pads to Walt's chest while Gabe charged the defibrillator. For Pete, it was surreal to watch the drama from the other side. Physically and emotionally drained from the events of the day, he knew it was best to keep out of the way while his partner worked. The familiar crescendo tone of the defibrillator penetrated the room. Gabe applied the paddles to Walter's chest and delivered 200 Joules of electricity to his heart. Walt's arms flailed, his back arched and within seconds, he awakened. His heart returned to a regular rhythm with many extra beats. Gabe ordered lidocaine IV and the extra beats disappeared. At first, Walt was confused and combative. After a few minutes, Pete calmed and partially reoriented Walt.

Dr. Cato arrived at the same time as Clay and Walter's family. Gabe Paulson and Clint Cato discussed the situation while Pete went to the waiting room to explain what had happened.

Clay made a quick visit to let Walter know that he was there for him, but Walt was still in a fog from his brief cardiac arrest. Pete and Clay walked with Walt as they wheeled him to the cath lab. While Dr. Cato worked on Walt, Pete and Clay strolled to a secluded gazebo at the side of the hospital.

"What kind of chance does he have?" Clay said soberly.

"I thought he was a goner when he went into the bad rhythm in the ER. It's a good thing he was right there on a monitor when it happened or he would be dead. Now that he's in the cath lab, he has an excellent chance for full recovery."

"Is it true that you just came across him by chance, Pete?"

"Yeah. I was sneaking out the back way to avoid the vultures from the newspaper when I found him on the stairs. He was headed home. If all that commotion had not happened in the ER today, I wouldn't have gone down those stairs."

"It's funny how these things work out. You had quite a day. Are you doing OK?"

"It's very hard to watch a teenager die. This will be with me until *I* die. I'm trying to put it in perspective. Vickie and I had a nice talk afterward and I feel much better."

"Vickie told me that your talk afterward was a big help for her, too. You know she thinks the world of you."

"I feel the same way about Vickie. More than any other nurse I've worked with, she and I seem to be on the same wavelength most of the time. She's quite a gal."

"I'm just starting to learn that. So, what's with your aversion to talking to the newspaper? Most docs I know love that time in the limelight."

"I've had a general mistrust of the media since I got burned once. When I was on the foundation board in Maryland, we had a sticky issue. A local widow gave a ton of money to the foundation. The family challenged it in court. When the local paper called me for an interview, they asked me the amount of the gift. I knew the amount but I wasn't going to tell them. They made up some figure that was way off and quoted me on it. I spent the next week explaining my way out of it. Never again. So, what did you do off the island today?"

"I went to see an attorney in Savannah."

Before Clay could continue, Pete's beeper alarmed.

"It's the ER. They should have news."

Pete and Clay hurried up the steps to the ER to find Dr. Cato conversing with Gabe Paulson.

"What can you tell us, Clint?" asked Clay.

"Great news. He had a single blockage of the left anterior descending artery. I opened it up with the balloon and placed a stent. He's got good flow and seems to have excellent heart function now. He'll be in the ICU overnight because of the rhythm problems he had earlier. He should be home in three or four days, and probably back to work in two or three weeks."

"Thanks, Clint. Old Walter means quite a bit to us," said Clay.

"A lot of credit also goes to these two guys. If Pete hadn't convinced him to come and if Gabe hadn't treated his arrhythmia so quickly, it would be a different story. We're lucky to have you guys here."

Pete and Gabe nodded to each other. They enjoyed the compliment not only for itself but also for its rarity. Pete knew that in emergency medicine, good deeds usually go unnoticed or at least unacknowledged while problems are often run up the medical staff flagpole. It was a good day indeed and they savored it, if only briefly.

Pete found Walt sleeping soundly in the ICU. Sugar and saline solution dripped in one arm while medication dripped into the other. The monitor displayed a normal blood pressure and a nice regular heart rhythm. A catheter bag half full of urine hung from the side of the bed. Pete pulled an uncomfortable yellow lounge chair next to the bed and quickly drifted off to sleep. Walter did not stir until 2 a.m., when he awakened confused. Pete reoriented him and explained what happened. The brief cardiac arrest had caused him to have some amnesia. Pete recounted the events of the evening for Walter and convinced the nurse to remove the urinary catheter before Walt fell back asleep. Pete awakened again at 7:15 a.m. to the sound of Walter eating his breakfast.

"That's a good sign—you have an appetite."

"Thanks for everything you did yesterday. I owe my life to you."

"We both owe each other quite a bit. Not about to start keeping track now. You're lucky I came by."

"It was more than luck."

"How so?" Pete said, as he stood and stretched.

"God's grace."

"I don't know. Don't put much stock in divine intervention."

"How many times you been down those stairs to go home at night?"

"Just the once."

"Think about that for a spell. We'll talk again."

CHAPTER 18

▼

Tami Bennett sat at the head of an enormous mahogany table in the boardroom of Hilton Head Hospital. Pete felt that her condescending and controlling demeanor was out of place for a philanthropic organization. She breezed through the routine agenda items with little enthusiasm. If it weren't for her amplified cleavage, half the male board members would be asleep. A portly and unfashionably dressed Larry Carver sat next to her. From the start, Pete thought there was something fishy about Carver. He just couldn't put his finger on it. Minutes from the previous meeting received uninterested approval from the group of 10 other trustees. As usual, there was no old business to cover. Carver, the poster child for boring and aging accountants, gave a bland and incomprehensible review of the financial information. None of the trustees had any significant financial background, so the report was more of a formality.

New business consisted of a rubber stamp of approval to provide the hospital board with funds to buy a new anesthesia machine for the operating room. Pete thought it strange that the board members were not better stewards of the funds. *What's wrong with the old anesthesia machine? Could this money be better spent elsewhere?* They all knew the routine and nobody was interested in upsetting it. The board requested money and they provided it.

Tami Bennett then formally introduced Pete as the newest member of the foundation board. She gave a brief review of his credentials as a physician and his foundation experience in Maryland. Henry Volk, a retired surgeon from New York state, took the opportunity to learn how other foundations operate. Prior to coming to Hilton Head, Volk had little philanthropic experience and knew little of these matters.

"Peter, I was wondering about how the finances were handled in your foundation in Maryland. Could you tell us about your experience there?"

"First, I'd like to thank you for the warm welcome y'all have given me." A few southern expressions had already crept into Pete's vocabulary. "I look forward to serving with you. I can tell you about the foundation but I'm not sure that it will apply directly here. The foundation in Maryland is a community foundation, and it functions much differently than this one. Grant applications are taken every quarter, and grants are made based on funds available and the worthiness of the request. Here we provide funds for only one entity so things are much simpler."

"What about the accounting?" chimed Volk.

Tami shot a look over to Carver that went right through him and the wall behind him.

"Because it is a much larger foundation, we had a full-time accounting and development staff. The accountant gave regular reports, as Mr. Carver does, and an independent firm audited our books annually."

"Thanks for that informative bit of information, Dr. Fredericks," Tami said quickly.

"Hold on, I'm not done yet," Volk injected. He continued to look at Pete and ignored Tami. Tami rolled her eyes at Carver. "I'm not raising this issue to question Mr. Carver. I want everyone to understand that," qualified Volk. "Larry, do we do any kind of independent review of the books each year?"

"No," Carver said tersely. "We've always felt our small foundation didn't need the large expense."

"The cost is excessive and I've never seen the need for it," added Tami Bennett. "So if there is no other new business, I—"

"I'm not done with *this* business, Madam Chairman," Volk retorted.

"I apologize. Please continue, Doctor."

Beads of sweat formed on Tami's chest and ran between her breasts, the plastic surgeon's version of the Grand Canyon. She shifted in her chair and tapped her Mont Blanc pen on her yellow legal pad.

"It seems to me that for everyone's protection as trustees, we should have our books reviewed periodically. It can't cost *that* much. Does anyone else have any feelings on this?"

Surprised but pleased by the rare excitement, several others, including Pete, chimed in supporting Volk. One sheep strays from the group and then they all start bleating and wandering away.

"I think it's a fine idea, Henry," Pete said, giving him the thumbs-up sign. "I think state law requires it in Maryland."

Big mistake. Never say 'that's the way we did it in Maryland' when you move to the South. Tami stood to remove her jacket and leaned forward on the table.

"Dr. Fredericks. You'll soon learn that none of us here cares too much about how things are done in the great state of Maryland."

"I care," said Volk, as he stood up. If they had swords, he and Tami would have drawn them. "And I propose that Mr. Carver gets bids from three South Carolina accounting firms for a one-time review of our books for the last five years."

"Dr. Volk, we've been through this before and I feel that it is really not necessary. Larry Carver is quite competent to handle our matters," replied a clearly irritated Bennett. She shot a pleading look over to Carver.

"I'm not questioning Mr. Carver's ability or honesty. I just feel that this is the proper thing for us to do. We've heard from Dr. Fredericks that other foundations do this. If there's no more discussion, I think that we should vote on my proposal."

"Well, I've had my say. Does anyone else have comments before I call for the vote?" said Tami, nearly exasperated.

Pete wondered if this was too much boat rocking for his first meeting. *Too late now.* The proposal passed easily. What harm's a little accounting anyway? The meeting ended quickly after the vote. The usually calm and composed Tami Bennett left in a huff.

Pete found Clay and Walter in the step-down unit at the hospital.

"Hey, fellas. You're looking fit. So how do you feel, Walt?"

"Better than I have in weeks. Cato says I can go home tomorrow if my heart behaves tonight."

"Great news. I can't tell you how happy I am. Should be good for another 40 years now," Pete said with a broad smile.

"I was just on my way out," said Clay.

"Walt, I'll be back in a minute. I'll walk you down to your car and fill you in on the meeting."

Pete waited until they walked out of earshot from the nurse's station and then recounted events.

"Tami took it, let's say, poorly."

"It seems like a reasonable proposal to me," Clay said, shrugging his shoulders. Most foundations I know of have an annual outside review of the books. What did the Silicone Princess do?"

"I thought she was going to blow a gasket. Her face was flushed and she flew out of there like an alley cat caught in the garbage by a Rottweiler."

"The Bennetts run this place like it's their own little general store. They don't like having other people tell 'em what to do. I may or may not hear from Mort on this. He's hard to predict sometimes. I appreciate the heads-up. Don't worry about it. I'll see you in the morning for fishing."

CHAPTER 19

▼

He parked close to the pier and found the marina nearly deserted. Clay would have to fish alone because the ER called Pete to fix an urgent problem. Even on an unseasonably warm Saturday, few fishermen ventured out in December. Clay learned from Walter that the fish were still there in winter. You just had to look harder and in different spots. Even if he didn't get a bite, Clay knew that he would enjoy a day in the sun and fresh air. He could forget about budgets, Betts, and board meetings.

Clay still couldn't throw the bait net well enough to catch mullet so he walked to the marina to get some shrimp. He knew Walt would disapprove, but since he wasn't there to complain, Clay didn't care. He wasn't going to fall into the cold water just to brag to Walt about bait.

"It's nice to see somebody's goin' out to enjoy this fine day," the marina owner said.

"Yeah, somebody's got to do it and I'm the man," Clay said with feigned pride.

"Where ya headed today, Clay?"

"The whole day's ahead of me, so I'm gonna head to the south side of Dau-fuski, and try my luck there."

The day and his whole life were a head of him. Clay never had so much energy for life and, at the same time, so much peace. He still missed his wife, but life was treating him well and he relished it. He had never run in such a small circle of friends and yet enjoyed such close friendships. He found what was important in life. Or did it find him?

He loaded his gear onto the skiff and stowed it. He pulled a Diet Coke from the cooler and placed it in the cup holder. He adjusted his sunglasses and hat, and turned the key. An explosion, which broke the silence of a clear Hilton Head morning, also shattered the windows of the marina. Pieces of fiberglass and metal fired in all directions, impaling the sides of nearby boats. Debris streamed high in the air like a bizarre fireworks display. The stern of the boat destroyed, the engine and gasoline tank plunged 70 feet to the bottom of the waterway, leaving only a multicolored film of gasoline on the water. The boat quickly filled with water. Clay's mangled body, which had blasted into and over the center console, lay motionless near the bow, face down in the water. Still moored, the boat listed away from the pier.

With blood running down his face and arms, the owner of the marina ran to Clay's boat. Shards of glass had gashed several large lacerations. He dialed 911 on his cellular phone. Fire, police, and EMS converged on the marina over a 10-minute period. All the responders felt helpless. There was no fire. There were no criminals to pursue. There was only the marina owner to help. Clay was dead. His face and chest were crushed by the injury, and he died before he hit the water. There were obvious multiple long-bone fractures and the side of his skull was flattened, causing a mortal brain injury. Futilely, an EMT checked for a pulse.

After Sheriff Gibby Morgan surveyed the scene, EMS pulled Clay's body from the boat. The air was still thick with the odor of burnt fiberglass and gasoline fumes as a small crowd of onlookers gathered. The EMT zipped Clay into the black body bag to await the coroner, who was on his way from Beaufort to collect the body for an autopsy. Later, they pulled what was left of the boat to the hoist and lifted it from the water. Gibby had neither the resources nor the desire to fish the engine from the murky depths.

EMS transported the marina owner to the hospital for treatment of his lacerations. Pete and Vickie had been discussing a policy problem in the trauma room when word arrived. Pete could barely grasp the news.

"How could this happen? Are you sure he's dead?" Pete pleaded to the EMT.

"I'm sorry, doc. Checked the pulse myself."

A dark feeling came over him. Pete's life had been so deficient of a loving father and Clay was beginning to help fill the void. He wondered why Clay and why now? Pete saw Vickie lean against the stretcher with her face in her hands, sobbing and shaking. He knew that he would need to put his grief aside long enough to get her out of the ER. He helped her back to his office and sat her on the bed.

"I'm so sorry. I know you loved each other."

Pete sat beside her and held her hand for a few minutes. "Sit here. I need to find Walt. I'll come back to get you."

Pete took the back steps down to the maintenance area. The nurses told Pete that Walt wanted to pick something up from his work area before going home. He found Walt sitting in his raggedy swivel chair with his forearms resting on his knees. Pete could tell from Walt's face.

"You heard?"

"Yeah."

"I'm so sorry, Walt. You guys were like brothers."

"We *were* brothers," Walt said, as he hung his head.

Pete sat on Walt's desk and let him grieve for a while. He thought about how Clay had filled the lives of people at the hospital. What a shame.

"I'm gonna drive you and Vickie to your place, OK?"

Walt nodded as Pete ran back upstairs to get Vickie. A funerary mood hung over the hospital like the fog of a damp January morning. Word spread rapidly through the hospital and, by afternoon, most of the small island knew of the tragedy. The nurses, clerks, and technologists at the hospital felt intense grief. In his short tenure, Clay had energized these employees who felt a great kinship with him. Not only did his employees hold him in high regard, but they also genuinely liked him. During an era of overpaid and arrogant executives, Clay was truly a rarity.

Molly, Pete, Vickie, and Walter sat on Walter's back deck and talked for several hours. An afternoon storm rumbled in the distance. Pete felt the chill. They cried and laughed and told stories. He could sense Walter's enormous loss. It showed on his weathered face. Pete had never seen Walter so sad, yet at the same time, he seemed at peace.

CHAPTER 20

▼

Clay lay in a simple wooden closed casket near the altar of the Presbyterian Church. An open casket was not desired or possible. Flowers surrounded him. An arrangement of lilies rested on the altar. Clay's family sat in the first two rows. Pete, Molly, Victoria, and Walter sat in the third row. A crowd of mourners overflowed the church. The balcony filled. Folding chairs lined the outer aisles. Eventually, the latecomers could stand only in the vestibule. Carver stood in the back corner by himself. Betts was a no-show.

Walter slowly took his place at the lectern. He stood quietly for a moment and gazed over the solemn group.

"I am Walter Ferguson, friend and employee of Clayton Jeffrey Stevens. I welcome you into God's house to celebrate the life and mark the passing of our dear friend, Clay."

"Clay was an important man in the eyes of God and in the eyes of his fellow man. He raised two wonderful children with his wife, Mary. He was responsible for runnin' several different organizations with big budgets and many employees. He served on the boards of corporations and charities. Yes indeed, Clay was a *very* important man. But, you would *never* know it to talk to him."

"The first day I met Clay, I didn't know him from Adam. He came down to the maintenance area at the hospital wearing jeans and a work shirt. Clay introduced himself and struck up a conversation with me about fishin'. He said he was new and didn't know the waters. I told him that I'd be happy to go fishin' with him any time. We talked for about half an hour about Hilton Head Island and the hospital and about me. He was very interested in knowin' about *me*. He wanted to know how I liked workin' at the hospital and what it was like to grow up on Hilton Head. Eventually, he asked me to do him a favor. He had some boxes to bring in and he was hopin' I had a hand truck he could borrow. I told him that I would not only give him a hand truck, but I would help him carry his load. We talked more as we walked to the parking lot in front of the administration offices. We unloaded some boxes from his car and he led me to the CEO's office. It wasn't until then that I realized who I was talkin' to."

"To this day, I never met the CEO of Hilton Head Hospital. I only met my good friend and fishin' buddy, Clay. During our friendship, we helped each other carry our burdens of life. We shared simple pleasures of fishing or watching the sunset from my back yard. We shared our pains and our joys. Clay was everything a friend should be. He accepted me for what I am and for what I am not. Clay always offered more in our relationship than he took away."

"Some of you may know that I nearly died recently and spent a short time in the hospital. I thank God I stand before you today. Clay came to work very early on the mornin' I went home from the hospital. He came to my room and he sat with me and we talked. He told me how much I meant to him. He told me that he loved me, and I told Clay that I love him. I am grateful that I had the opportunity to share my feelings with Clay before he left us. I knew that we were good friends. He didn't need to tell me he loved me. I knew it. I'm so glad that he did, though. It meant so much then and so much now. I hope that I will always remember to tell my friends and loved ones what they mean to me. Clay taught me a valuable lesson that day."

"Our friend is gone now. And how shall we bear this heavy load? Listen to the words of the Lord."

> *Come to me, all you who are weary and burdened, and I will give you rest. Take my yoke upon you and learn from me, for I am gentle and humble in heart and you will find rest for your souls. For my yoke is easy and my burden is light.*

"Clay has left us, but he lives on in all those who know him. His kind and loving nature was contagious. Remember him by living his example of friendship. Carry a burden for a friend. And should that burden become too heavy, you know where to turn. May the grace of God be with you all."

Most wept as Walter stepped down and sat next to Pete. Walter sat stone faced. His simple story told with his easy drawl crystallized Clay's life for Pete. This comforted him and a serene feeling came over him. Two of Walter's brothers sang an a capella duet of *Swing Low Sweet Chariot*. Their deep, soft voices moved Pete. The pastor completed the service and gave the benediction. The service closed with *Amazing Grace*. The sound was bittersweet.

Later that day, their dear friends from New Orleans, Wade and Debbie Boudreaux, arrived. Debbie was dying of breast cancer. She had been through two rounds of chemotherapy and one round of radiation therapy. Bald and 20 pounds lighter, the cancer was killing her, bit by bit. The last set of tests showed it had spread to her brain. Molly and Debbie had maintained a close friendship since grade school. The purpose of this trip was not just a friendly visit. Debbie had come to see Dr. Wilhelm Betts the following week.

During the course of visits to each other's houses and joint vacations, Pete and Wade had become close as well—probably closer than their wives. Debbie worked as a nurse at Charity Hospital in New Orleans. Wade, 10 years older than Debbie, took his retirement from the FBI. Never one to sit still, Wade built a successful private investigation agency as a second career. There was no shortage of dirt to gather for people in the Big Easy. Working for the wife, Wade had recently exposed the extramarital affair of a city councilman. It was a good time to be out of the city.

The couples enjoyed a wonderful dinner at Le Bistro on the first night of the visit. After dinner, they drove to the beach to enjoy a stroll and the warm evening. The girls walked 20 yards behind as Pete recounted recent events to Wade. Wade stood 6 feet 4 inches and weighed 225 pounds. Quite solid and muscular, he continued to maintain fitness requirements from his days in the FBI. He sported a full head of black hair and a rugged face that bore battle scars from work as a street cop in New Orleans. He left the police department for the FBI because of the top-to-bottom corruption in the NOPD. Wade earned honors and the respect of his fellow agents during his tenure at the Bureau.

"So what kinda boat did the CEO have?" inquired Wade, in his flavorful Cajun drawl.

"A simple outboard center-console skiff. Kept it in excellent condition."

"Oh yeah. I know that skiff. That boat great for gettin' 'round in the bayou. Don't draw much water. Good for 'gator huntin' too. You know much about boat engines?"

"Enough to know where de gas and de oil goes," said Pete, mimicking Wade's accent. Why?"

"Outboard engines don't explode like you say. Inboard engines can explode if the fumes build up in the bilge. Outboard engines just don't have that problem."

"So what are you saying?"

"Somethin' else had to be on that boat to explode. He keep any extra fuel cans might've leaked?"

"No way. Clay was very meticulous about that type of thing. He would wipe up gasoline drips with a rag."

"Any enemies?"

"Not that I know of here. Maybe back in Charleston."

"He was out of the picture in Charleston, wasn't he?"

"I guess so."

"Makes more sense it would be someone on the island. Any kind of controversy going on at the hospital? Was he sideways with somebody?"

Pete realized where Wade was headed. *This is ridiculous. What possibly could be going on at the hospital to make somebody want to kill Clay? This is a little hospital on a little island stuck on the edge of a little state. Wade's imagination is getting the best of him.*

"There's always controversy at a hospital. CEOs have to make tough decisions. I'm sure he pissed off someone, but I doubt it was enough to make someone want to kill him. The only thing that would come even close to that is the controversy over Dr. Betts."

"The guy we came to see."

"Right," Pete said, "I told you I couldn't completely vouch for him."

Pete briefed Wade on the Betts situation and the plan to do peer review of some of his cases.

"They do anything?"

"No, the whole thing will go to the back burner for a while."

"This doctor upset about the quality review?"

"I don't see the guy too much. You wouldn't know it the few times I talked to him."

"Who put up a fuss about it?"

"Chairman of the board, Lieutenant Colonel Bennett. Clay said he gave him a bit of a hard time about Betts."

"Morton Bennett?"

"Know him?" asked Pete, with a surprised look on his face.

"Just of him. He was the target of an investigation when he was stationed at Parris Island. They never indicted him, but the investigators figured he was funnelin' cash to himself. We checked out a few leads from our office. Never linked it to him. Somebody did some slick accountin' on that base. Higher ups killed the investigation. He took his retirement when the heat was off."

"Who was the head of accounting at the base?" said Pete, starting to become suspicious himself.

"Do I look like I got some kinda photographic memory?

"Actually you look kinda retarded. I wasn't gonna say anything, but since you asked," Pete joked, as he put a hand on Wade's shoulder.

"You pretty sharp for a dumb Yankee. Anyway, I might know the name if I heard it, but I don't got it in my head."

"Try Larry Carver on for size."

"Where'd you get Larry Carver?" Wade said, perplexed.

"He's the accountant at the hospital."

"Now we gettin' somewhere. He's the accountant from Parris Island. What else he do for Bennett?"

"He's the accountant for the hospital foundation I'm on."

"And what else?"

Maybe it was the alcohol at dinner or lack of sleep. Pete felt lightheaded and wanted to sit down, but he didn't want the girls to catch up to them. *This is crazy. Even if those two embezzled from the Marines, who's to say they're doing it now.* They paced on as Pete wiped his brow.

"That's all I know."

"Back up now. You on this foundation?"

"Yeah. Bennett's sister is the chairman."

"And what'd you do to piss them off at the foundation?"

"Why do you ask?" said Pete, slow to catch on to Wade's theory.

"Didn't you say you were supposed to fish with Clay that day?"

"Yeah. I got called in to work."

"Pete, they were tryin' to kill you, too."

"Shhhh, not so loud. I don't want Molly to get upset about this. Look Wade, I find it hard to believe anybody wanted to kill me."

"OK, just think about this a minute. What was happenin' at the foundation?" Wade said, in a low voice.

"We voted to have the books audited," whispered Pete.

"They do it yet?"

"No, we haven't met since."

"They tryin' to kill two birds with one stone. We need to get into Carver's office and find out what he's been up to. Your life may depend on it."

Lightheaded didn't describe it well any more. *Swimming. That's it.* If Pete didn't sit down soon, he was going to collapse on the beach. All this talk of murder, the alcohol, and the girls' closing in on them was more than he wanted for an after-dinner stroll on the beach.

"I don't know. Why don't we just call the police? This whole idea sounds pretty far-fetched to me."

"They barely checked out the explosion. They not gonna do shit with this. We need in Carver's office. There's got to be more to it," urged Wade.

"That's going to be tough. I'd rather not end up in jail on a breaking and entering charge."

"All right, put that aside a minute. Think back to the weeks before Clay's death. What else was goin' on?"

"Clay was very close to one of my ER nurses. They were spending a lot of time together. Only a few of us knew about it."

"She have an ex-husband?"

"Yeah, but he's been out of the picture for a while."

"We need to meet with her—tonight."

"She's probably at home."

"OK. Let's take the girls home. Tell them that I want to see where you work. We'll see what she's got for us."

As they drove to Vickie's, Pete briefed Wade on Victoria and her relationship with Clay. Vickie gave Pete a hug and a peck on the cheek as they entered her condo. Pete introduced Wade as the best Cajun detective this side of the Mississippi.

"So what's up? Certainly you're not out at this hour just to jaw with me."

"As a matter of fact, we are. I don't want to upset you, but Wade has some information to suggest that Clay was murdered."

They settled into wicker chairs on her balcony that overlooked the marsh. A cool evening breeze carried the semi-sweet smell of marsh at low tide. Pete chilled as the sweat evaporated.

"I can't believe this. I thought that this was investigated completely by the police. What's this all about?"

Pete recounted his discussion with Wade. Vickie listened intently. There were no tears or sad faces, only determination.

"Is there anything Clay told you in the days or weeks before his death you think might help us?" Wade asked gently.

"Remember the day Walter got sick?"

"I won't soon forget it," said Pete, as he pulled a beach towel from the back of the chair around his shoulders.

"What I mean is—you remember Clay saying he had been off the island that day?"

"Yeah, I guess."

"Did he tell you what he did that day?"

"No, too much commotion with Walt."

"He went to see an attorney in Savannah to get a handle on his options. He learned the week before that someone had hired a private investigator to dig up dirt on him."

Wade shrugged innocently. "We not all scumbags."

"A friend from Charleston had called to tell him someone was nosing around. Clay wanted to know how he could legally find out who had hired the PI. He told me he thought it was Bennett, but needed to be able to prove it to do him any good."

"So what'd the attorney tell him?" prodded Wade.

"Don't know. They were supposed to meet again. I hoped to ask the attorney the other day but it didn't seem appropriate," said Vickie.

"You met with the lawyer?" asked Wade, with a curious look on his face.

"I'm sorry. I'm confusing you. They read Clay's will the other day. He had just made a new will with this attorney. I don't know if he thought they might kill him or if it was just a convenient time to take care of it," said Vickie.

"Can you think of anything else that he may have said or done?"

"I know he was a little spooked about Bennett. He didn't care for Bennett or his sister. He called them phonies. He wondered how a military man came into so much money. I can't think of anything else."

"So Pete, do you need any more information to make a decision about this?" cajoled Wade.

"We'll see. Let me sleep on it."

"Sleep on what?" asked Vickie.

"We're just trying to figure out what to do next," said Pete, wanting to keep Wade's burglary plan quiet.

CHAPTER 21

▼

Enjoying the last few days of the Easter recess, Buddy Duke sat on the side veranda of his historic home in the Battery District of Charleston. With his back to the street, he gently rocked his wooden chair and shot the breeze with Dick Coswell. A horse-drawn carriage with a guide and four tourists clopped by. His wife huddled with her staff in the dining room to coordinate the last details for a cocktail party scheduled for that evening. Coswell answered the secure cell phone on the first ring and he walked to the parlor at the front of the house.

"Red Line."

"Dick, it's Gibby Morgan."

"Are you close by?" Coswell murmured.

"Yeah."

"Good. Pull around to the side entrance and pick me up."

Gibby and Carver made the quick trip up to Charleston to explain in person what happened to Clay Stevens. Both expected an earful from Coswell who got in the back seat carrying a glass with whiskey on ice.

"Why don't you drive while we talk?"

"Dick, I'm sorry for the screw up," offered Carver.

"I thought your plan was to scare this fella Stevens," Coswell said, sounding much more concerned about the impact on him and the campaign than any remorse about Clay.

"This is really all my fault. I overestimated the charge on the explosive," Gibby said.

"Forget it. Water under the bridge. Right now we need to concentrate on keeping a lid on this damn mess. Hopefully with Stevens gone, this nonsense with Betts is over. We still need to make this foundation problem go away. Gibby, you need to scare the crap out of the troublemakers on the foundation board. You've got the imagination for this kind of shit. Do what you want. Try not to kill anybody else."

"No problem," Gibby said, looking down in remorse.

"Larry, keep me up to speed now. We want to get rid of little problems early before they become big ones," Coswell said. "I don't want this campaign derailed before it leaves the station."

CHAPTER 22

▼

Pete, Molly, Wade, and Debbie boarded the tour boat at Harbour Town. A red and white lighthouse stood guard over the shops and the semicircular marina. Being early in the season, only a few sailboats were moored. The excursion boat made daily trips to the riverfront area of Savannah. They walked to the top deck of the red and white 60-foot craft to enjoy the sunshine. Sitting on newly painted benches, they traded stories as they waited for the crew to cast off. The deep hum of the accelerating engines caused a group of gulls to lift from the outer railing. They could feel the vibration of the huge diesel engines through the bench. Bottlenose dolphin swam near the bow as they made the 45-minute trip. A few sailboats dotted the ocean near the horizon. Pete marveled at the view of Savannah as they navigated north on the Savannah River. Untouched in the War of Northern Aggression—as some liked to say—many historic buildings stood very well preserved.

The girls headed off to shop and left the boys with nebulous plans to *look around*. As soon as their wives passed out of sight, Wade and Pete walked to the office of Hutson "Buster" Davidson. Only in the South, would an attorney using the nickname Buster reach such a level of prominence in the community. Buster headed a medium-sized firm that practiced mostly contract and estate law. They followed Abercorn Street to State Street, and found the office in a restored building between Wright Square and Telfair Square. Approximately 20 squares like these gave Savannah its unique southern charm and character. They found an expansive mahogany staircase in the center of the first-floor lobby, and took it to the offices that occupied the entire third floor. After a 20-minute wait, a sophisticated-looking, long-legged secretary admitted them to the large corner office of

Hutson Q. Davidson, Esq. A large picture window provided a pleasant view of Johnson Square. A short, white-haired man with a thick white mustache emerged from behind an antique wooden desk. Appearing to be in his 50s, Buster wore a seersucker suit and black cowboy boots. He spoke in a gruff voice—sort of a Yosemite Sam with a brief case. He introduced himself and offered them a seat in large wing chairs that surrounded a coffee table in the corner of the office.

"What can I do for you gents today?" smiled Buster.

"First, we'd like to thank you for seein' us on short notice," said Wade. "As we spoke on the phone, we have reason to think that your client, Clay Stevens, was murdered. We're hopin' you could tell us about your meetin' with him."

"Since you're after a murderer here, I'll bend the rules a bit. I *will* ask you gentleman to keep this discussion in confidence. This meeting never took place. Is that understood?" he said, with a stern look.

"Yes, sir," in unison.

"OK. Mr. Stevens had reason to believe the scumbag Morton Bennett had put a private Dick on his trail. I told him we could sic one of our investigators on the other investigator and find out what he was up to. I also told him there was no law against someone having him investigated."

"What did Clay want to do?" asked Pete, after shooting a glance over to Wade. *So that's what you are. Private Dick.*

"He wasn't sure he wanted to get into the expense of a private investigation. Was gonna think about it. We made out a new will for him. He hadn't done anything since his wife died. Had the reading here a few days ago. Nice family."

"Did he say if he was concerned about being murdered?" Wade said.

"No. It was more of a routine thing. He mentioned the will almost in passing." Davidson walked to his desk to light a cigar, not asking if anyone cared. He leaned against the edge of his desk with his boots crossed.

"Why did he come here rather than Beaufort or Charleston?" asked Wade.

"We belong to the South Carolina Bar and do lots of work for folks on Hilton Head. People come here because they know their personal business won't become cocktail party babble on Hilton Head."

"What about this investigator?" prodded Wade.

"We did a preliminary check just to find any red flags. His name is Rodney Wilkes. Licensed investigator in South Carolina among a few other states. Don't know who hired him. No outstanding warrants and never been arrested," Buster said, as he thumbed through the file. "He's had a few speeding tickets and pays court-ordered alimony to an ex-wife in Kentucky. Didn't find much else. Far as we can tell, Wilkes was talking to friends and associates of Mr. Stevens under the guise he was doing a story for a local magazine. One of those 'Where are they now?' kind of things. A friend became suspicious about the line of questioning and called him."

Pete and Wade raised their eyebrows at each other, signaling it was time to go.

"Thank you for your time, Mr. Davidson," said Wade.

"By the way," said Pete, as they approached the door. "You called Bennett a scumbag. What makes you feel that way?"

"The general opinion here is that Bennett is dirty. A couple of our clients got screwed in some shaky deal with Bennett and that cancer doctor you got up there on fantasy island."

"Betts."

"Right. That's him."

"What can you tell us about the deal?" asked Wade.

"It involved Betts' lab. I can't tell you any details—*those* clients are still alive."

Pete and Wade came out to a clear and cloudless day. Both put on shades. A young black man in 19th-century attire walked by on his way to work at one of the nearby bed and breakfasts. A trim-looking young lady in a sweatshirt from the Savannah College of Art and Design walked a ragtag group of dogs.

"That's the link," said Wade, as they walked back to the riverfront. "Bennett is uptight about this thing with Betts 'cause he's got some kind of financial interest. When things don't make sense, follow the money."

"How can we find out more about this investigator?"

"I know an agent in the Charleston office of the Bureau. He owes me a big favor for gettin' him Super Bowl tickets at the Superdome a couple years ago. I should still have his cell phone number in my little brain here."

After switching his shades for bifocals, Wade pulled a small electronic organizer from his pocket and located the number for Marcus Fisher. He punched the numbers on his cell phone as they sat in front of the Savannah Hilton and enjoyed the view of the river.

"Marcus, it's Wade Boudreaux."

"What's new in the Big Easy, Cajun Man?"

"Nothin', I'm in Savannah."

"What in hell are you doing there?"

"A vacation to Hilton Head Island has turned into a little murder investigation. I want the dirt on a local PI."

"You gotta name? Maybe I know him."

"Rodney Wilkes."

"Never heard of him. Gimme a day or two to run him down and I'll see what I can do. What do you need from him?"

"He was investigating a guy named Clayton Stevens."

"Now, that name I've heard. Wasn't he some hotshot executive? They did his death on the local news here."

"Yeah, that's the guy. He was murdered. Find out who hired Wilkes, and I'll have Sugar Bowl tickets for you."

"That's quite an enticement, man. I may have to beat the crap out of ol' Rodney."

"Whatever it takes, Marcus. Just get the name."

Pete drank a root beer while Wade chatted. He thought about what a different world Wade works in. People often told Pete that they couldn't do his job. Pete knew he definitely could not do Wade's.

"Is this enough proof for you yet, honey?" Wade said, almost as a dare.

"I want to hear back from your man in Charleston before we dive into this thing. Just give me a little more time. You do this shit every day. I'm spooked by all of it. And look here, sweetie, I told you not to call me honey in public."

When the two couples returned home, Wade parked in the drive. Tired was not the word for it. Pete knew that as soon as he sat down, he would crash. As they walked in the front door, Pete noticed something hanging from the big live oak in the side yard. From a distance it looked like a blanket tossed over one of the twisting branches. He pulled the door shut without the others realizing that he didn't follow. He figured he would just pull it down before it got soaked in the rain forecast for that night. Pete's heart pounded as he came close enough to see his Irish Setter hanging by the neck from a live oak tree. Defeated and demoralized, Pete stood next to Sean, running his fingers through the soft crimson coat. After several minutes, he realized that he needed to cut him down before Molly came out. Wade found him cutting furiously with his pocket knife.

"Goddamn sons of bitches. I'm gonna kill 'em."

"Man, I'm sorry 'bout Sean. These are some sick individuals. Here, I'll hold him while you cut."

Wade gently lowered the dead dog onto the thick grass. "They sendin' us a message, friend."

Molly called from the backyard. "Pete. Have you seen Sean?"

"Oh, shit," Wade said under his breath.

Pete and Molly met at the corner of the house. He held her close. Molly could see Sean's body as Wade stood up.

"He's dead. Somebody hanged him from the tree. I'm sorry. I'm so sorry."

They walked to Sean, and Molly knelt over the limp dog, hugging him and wailing.

"Who could do such a thing?" she cried.

They all sat with Molly while she held Sean's head on her lap. Just when it seemed she would stop, another wave of sobbing would come. After a half hour or so, Debbie helped Molly inside. Pete removed Sean's collar while Wade retrieved a shovel. Neither said anything while they dug a hole in the backyard. Anger swelled inside Pete like never before. He pulled off his sweaty shirt, whipping it at the ground.

"Let's get these bastards."

CHAPTER 23

▼

The next day, Wade and Pete awoke early and hustled down to Walter's. On the way, Pete briefed Wade on Walt's connection to Clay.

"Do you think Walt will help us get into the CFO's office?"

"I think he would if it meant discovering if Clay was murdered. But I hate to get Walt involved in this. He'd lose his job if we were discovered. I don't want to put any pressure on him. What do we do if we get in there?"

"Carver must have some books or records of some type to connect him to Bennett. It's too much of a coincidence those two are here on Hilton Head."

"I couldn't make sense of accounting reports or company books if my life depended on it. If we steal them, we'll tip them off." He kicked a stone along the dirt road as they walked. "We need to read them in the office. Do you know anything about this kind of stuff?" Pete said, feeling overwhelmed by all the issues ahead of them.

"Not enough to help us. We need somebody who knows accountin' to go in with us. Any ideas?"

"Let me think on that for a minute."

They found Walter dressed for work, drinking his morning coffee in the back-yard. An egret winged over the tidal stream as they came around the side yard. Pete introduced Walter to Wade and brought him up to speed on their suspicions.

"We want to get in and out of Carver's office unnoticed," Pete said as he paced back and forth in front of Walt. "Want to flip through his books and put them back where we found them. But I don't want you to come with us. There's no need for you to risk your job. If you just give me the key, I'll make a copy. If we get caught, I'll tell them I copied it without your knowledge."

"That might be the safest way for *me*, but I need to go along to keep you two out of trouble," Walt said, as he sat and sipped his coffee. "Number one. Look at this key," Walt said, as he pulled his omnipresent key ring from his belt. "You can't copy this here key at the hardware. This is a special key that you can only get from a locksmith. You need to sign for it and know the password for the facility. Carver had all the locks in the administration area changed to this kind a few months after he started working at the hospital. Number two. Somebody needs to stand watch while you're in the office. I'm the man. I can make it look like I'm supposed to be there fixin' somethin'. If somebody comes along, I can act real natural like and steer him away from the office. Number three. If Carver was in on this, I want in on takin' him down."

"Sounds good, Walter," said an eager Wade, as he rubbed his hands together. "You the man. We got one other problem. We don't want to steal the books. Just want to look at them. Don't want anybody knowin' we were there. We can't depend on bein' able to copy 'em. Pete and I don't know accountin'. I'm assumin' you don't either."

"Got that right," nodded Walter.

"You and Pete need to put on your thinking caps and come up with an accountant that's willin' to put himself on the line for us."

"Rick Dawson," said Walter, without a thought.

"What's a real estate agent know about accounting?" asked Pete, forgetting his previous conversation with Rick.

"Dawson was an accountant when he lived in Columbia," replied Walt, as he motioned for the two to take a seat.

"Do you think that he'll help us, Walt?" asked Wade.

"I think so. He's told me about some crazy things he's done. I don't think he'd be all that worried about a thing like this. He owes a debt to Clay for all the business he referred. You want me to call him?" offered Walt.

That evening Pete, Walter, Wade Boudreaux, and Rick Dawson met at Walter's. They sat around a wooden table in the kitchen, which showed the wear of 100 years of use by the Ferguson clan. Walter lived in a modest home that he kept it in excellent condition. The 20-year-old appliances in his kitchen shone and worked like new. Walter laid on a fresh coat of paint inside and out every three years. His wooden floors, although faded from foot traffic and sunlight, held a fresh coat of wax hand rubbed by Walter. Wade, being the professional in these matters, led the meeting.

Wade stood and leaned forward with his thick hands flat on the kitchen table. He summarized events for the group. The investigation of Clay. Bennett and Carver's relationship. Speculation about involvement with Betts. "I think that there is more. They planned to kill Pete along with Clay Stevens. We haven't found the link yet. The key to all this may be in Carver's office. We can't leave any trace that we were there. That's where you come in, Rick. We need you with us to decipher what's in his office."

"What do you think we'll find?" wondered Rick.

"Hopefully we'll find books relatin' to Betts' operation and the hospital foundation."

"It could take me hours to get through information like that. It would be easier if we could just copy it and look at it later," offered Rick.

"I have a camera and we can use the photocopier in the administration area if we need to," Walt reassured. We still need you to tell us what to copy. There's no tellin' what we're goin' to come across. We could miss somethin' important. We also need you to do a little searchin' through his computer. What do you say?"

"I'm always up for a little adventure," Rick said, with a devious grin.

"When should we do this, Walt?" asked Pete.

"Evening time, after the hospital visitors go home. I'm still there late sometimes so it won't seem unusual. If we can be out before 10:45, we'll miss the 11:00 change of shift of the nurses. Visitors are out by 9:00. If we plan to get there by 9:15, we'll have 90 minutes to do the job. How about night after tomorrow?"

"Sounds good to me," said Wade. "Sooner the better. Let's do this before they try to hang Pete from an oak tree."

Pete didn't like being reminded that someone might be looking to kill him. He could only blame himself for getting into such a conundrum. *Life in Maryland wasn't that bad. Now my dog is dead, and my job and my life are in jeopardy. Be careful what you wish for.*

Wade reviewed some standard procedures. "We'll all get coveralls like Walt so we look like a maintenance crew. Sneakers and double knot the laces. Baby powder under the insoles so they don't squeak. Cotton gloves. Walt, you're goin' to drive to the hospital and go to the maintenance area like you're comin' in to do some repair or somethin'. Think of somethin' to fix. Pete and Rick, once we're in, don't touch anything you don't have to. Pete, you and I will concentrate on findin' books and ledgers and a safe while Rick gets into the computer. Rick, you bring a box of high density storage disks in case we need to copy some files. Make sure they are formatted. Are there windows in Carver's office?"

"Yeah. Great big one," Walt said, with outstretched arms. The good news is it faces the woods and there's vertical blinds."

Walt walked to the counter to get the coffee pot for refills.

"We gotta have a plan case we need to leave in a hurry. We'll park a car in a remote spot on the way to the hospital. We'll muddy up the back of Pete's car so the plate is covered. Same for your car, Rick. Got any ideas on where to park, Pete?"

The complexity of the plan began to sink in. Pete had no idea that so much planning was needed for something like this. He thought they would just walk in and do some poking around.

"Catholic Church's lot near the hospital. We can park behind the church. It'll be dark there, and we could run through the woods," Pete said, starting to think like a criminal.

"How far?" Wade asked.

"I'd say a hundred yards."

"When we get the gloves tomorrow, we'll get enough rope to run from the edge of the woods near the hospital to the edge of the woods near the car. If we have to, we can pick up the rope as we enter the woods and follow it. That way we won't need lights and we can move faster than whoever is chasing us. Any questions?"

Pete wasn't too excited about the chasing part. Chasing was definitely bad. Visions of tripping in the woods and having cuffs slapped on him came to mind.

"How likely is this chasing?" Pete asked, as he paced the room.

"Just precautions, just precautions," Wade reassured.

"How are we going to get into a safe?" asked Pete.

"It's good to see you're thinking ahead. I think you smarter already from livin' in Dixie. I had some experience with safe crackin'. I got a little device that turns these office safes into piggy banks. Five minutes and I'll be in."

"What if he uses a password to get his computer started?" asked Rick.

"Those passwords are great for keepin' your secretary out of your system. They no use against ol' Wade. I got a couple of special disks to get his system started. If we really want to screw the bastard, I'll leave a little Cajun virus on his system that'll make Windows lock up every time he hits the letter Q. The neat thing about it is the virus waits for another 50 keystrokes to lock up the system. He never figure it out."

"What about Walt if things go bad?" asked Pete. "He can't be running through the woods."

"I'll be fine."

"No you will not. I'm dead serious about this. If things start to go bad, you need to let yourself into one of the other offices or clear out of there. There is no reason for you to stick your neck out any further than you have already. I know you feel fine but you're not ready to run through the woods. For God's sake, you're still in cardiac rehab. Now, is it agreed that you bug out if things go bad?"

Walt's health was Pete's biggest concern. He began to regret involving Walt, but it was too late to rework the plan. The last thing he wanted was to give Walt another heart attack.

"OK, you know more about this than me. I'll do what you say."

"If anybody wants to back out, now is the time," said Wade. "The only thing you'd be guilty of is conspiracy to commit a crime and we'd never tell. So is everybody in?"

CHAPTER 24

▼

Pete, Rick, and Wade made an early trip to Wal-Mart to get supplies. Everything a thief could need was right there in one big store. Flashlights, gloves, rope, paint, coveralls, black athletic shoes, pre-formatted high-density computer disks, and duct tape. You can always use duct tape. They checked out in separate lines to avoid suspicion, and paid cash. From Wal-Mart, they drove to the Catholic Church.

Only birds could be heard in the rear of the church as Pete backed into a parking spot near the pines. Wade pulled a machete that he borrowed from Walter from the trunk of Pete's car. He cut a path through the vegetation while Pete laid down rope. They tied three 100-foot lengths together to reach the other side of the woods. Rick followed, covering the rope lightly with the ample supply of pine straw that blanketed the forest floor. As they neared the far side of the woods, they could see Larry Carver sitting at his desk. They sat and waited for him to leave the office.

"What a weasel," commented Pete. "Something about this guy always bothered me but I couldn't put my finger on it."

"This whole thing would be a lot easier if I just shot him from here. I could hit him right above his left ear," quipped Wade.

"Down boy," Pete said.

"I always get the urge to pee in situations like this," Rick said.

"Well be sure to go before we leave Walter's," warned Wade, as Rick emptied his bladder.

"If it's going to be a problem, I could put in a Foley catheter and we could hook it to a leg bag for you," said Pete.

"I'm sorry I said anything," said Rick as he zipped up his pants.

Carver left his office, allowing the trio to continue laying rope. Wade tied it to the base of a medium-sized pine and marked it with a blaze of orange paint. They walked briskly back to the car. As they drove off, Wade's cell phone rang.

"Marcus, lay it on me, man."

"I found Rodney Wilkes. What a slime ball. I barely had to threaten him and he gave it up. It's not much, though. He says he never had a name. They spoke on the phone several times. He gave me the number—843-555-3673. He says that he was paid in advance by a Western Union money transfer."

"Shit, all we've got is a phone number. Pete, you got a phone book in the car?"

"Yeah, in the glove box. It's one of those mini books they give you with your cell phone. You're welcome to it if you can read the microscopic print."

"Bennett has two N's and two T's?" said Wade, as he placed his bifocals on his face.

"Yeah."

"No match there. What's the first three numbers for the lines at the hospital?"

"689."

"Is that every number?"

"I'm pretty sure."

"No match there. Let's try Carver's home number," said Wade, as he flipped the pages. "Bingo, what an idiot. He goes to all the trouble to pay by Western Union and not give his name but he gives the guy his home phone. Good. I guess we already knew the answer but it's always nice to have a little confirmation."

CHAPTER 25

▼

Buddy Duke and Dick Coswell huddled in his office after a long day of Senate meetings and calls to constituents. Ambition to be president won out over the fatigue that was biting at his heels. His outward display of energy concealed his severe back pain. Buddy popped an OxyContin and washed it down with a swallow of whiskey that would make most men choke.

"How's the campaign fund lookin' this week?" Buddy asked, as he stood and arched his back.

"This back-door money from Betts' lab and from our friends on Hilton Head has us on solid ground. We're in good shape to start some real fundraising now."

Buddy put full faith in Coswell because he knew the ins and outs of presidential campaigns from previous experience. Buddy knew that fundraising and political campaigning could be dirty business—especially presidential campaigning. He was counting on Coswell to get dirty for him. He didn't really enjoy campaigning but he did enjoy holding office, and he was willing to work 16-hour days for the next three years in order to get to the White House.

"Thanks to your wife and the Hilton Head money, we are organized in all but Alaska and South Dakota. We'll start making phone calls soon, and the real money will start to flow. You'll need to plan on a trip out of state at least once a week starting after Memorial Day." Coswell laid his papers on the desk and looked Buddy square in the eye. "This will be much harder that any Senate campaign. Are you up for this?"

Even Coswell didn't know Buddy was seeing a psychologist, but Buddy got the gist of the question. Buddy knew Coswell was well aware of his weaknesses. He didn't take offense to the question from his old friend.

"I'm ready. I got a lot of energy. Plus you're gonna do all the hard work anyway."

They shared a good laugh, knowing that he was speaking the truth.

"I want you to keep tabs on what's happening with Betts on Hilton Head. We don't need any monkeys on our backs this early in the campaign."

"I'm on top of it. Don't give it another thought."

CHAPTER 26

▼

That afternoon, the phone rang at Larry Carver's house. Since Wilkes had sold out Carver, he needed to make it appear that he had no choice. The machine picked up.

"It's Wilkes. FBI is on your trail about Stevens. They got your number off my phone records."

Larry Carver called Gibby Morgan immediately after listening to the message that evening.

"We need to talk."

"The usual place in 30 minutes," Gibby said.

Carver and Gibby took care to never be seen together outside public functions. One never went to the other's house, and they never discussed business on the telephone. The two would always meet in the evening in the parking lot near the marina. Gibby found Carver sitting in his Chevy Impala at the edge of the lot. As usual, Gibby got into the passenger seat of Carver's car. Carver was sweating and he looked pale.

"There was a message on my answering machine from Rodney Wilkes. He's the PI we used to dig up dirt on Stevens. He says that the FBI is looking into Stevens' death and they got my number off his phone records."

"Shit. Now how in hell could the damn FBI get involved in this?" Gibby said, scratching his round head. "And how would they know about Wilkes?"

"I have no damn idea," lamented Carver. "Do you want me to call him?"

"Hell no. They'll be lookin' for you to do that. No more contact with Wilkes. So what if we investigated Stevens. They can't tie us to his death. Contacting Wilkes now will only call attention to you. Let them look into it all they want.

It'll be a dead end. What I wanna know is who on Hilton Head is sticking their nose in this."

"Any ideas?" Carver said, deferring to Gibby's crime-fighting skills.

"Stevens' family lives out of state. They have no reason to suspect anything. I smooth talked them the day before the funeral. Who on the island was close to him?"

"He fished with Ferguson, the maintenance man at the hospital," offered Carver. "He doesn't seem like the type to be orchestrating some secret investigation into this."

"Who else?"

"Fredericks from the ER. He's one of them that's stirring up things at the foundation. He seems to be clueless that we were trying to get to him along with Stevens. There was a rumor around the hospital that Stevens had been doing one of the nurses from the ER—Victoria Jackson."

"What do you know about her?"

"Not much."

"See what you can find out without making anyone suspicious. Beep me on my pager if you need me. We need to stay off the phones now. Let me know if the FBI contacts you. Keep your eyes open for anything unusual at the hospital."

Gibby walked back to his pickup and waited for Carver to drive out of sight. He was in bed with Carver but he also knew where his ultimate allegiance would always be.

"Red line. Who's calling please?"

"Dick, it's Gibby."

"What's up?" Coswell said, as he drove to his home in Chevy Chase.

"FBI may be snooping around about Stevens. There's nothin' firm yet. I just thought that you would want to know about this kinda thing sooner rather than later."

"Thanks, Gibby. Let me know if you hear anything more. I'm going to remember this when we get to the White House."

After hanging up with Gibby, Coswell dialed up a friend who had connections to men skilled at solving sticky problems.

"Drew, it's Coswell. I need you to assemble a team to maybe do four hits down on Hilton Head. I'll let you know when it's a go for sure."

Coswell provided all the names, places, and other information needed to do the advance work. It would cost 10 thousand just to set it up. He looked at it as good insurance even if they didn't follow through with the plan.

CHAPTER 27

▼

"You boys are being awfully secretive," said Molly, as the two couples relaxed on the back porch. "What are you two plotting?"

"Who, us? Now what makes you think two good friends who ain't seen each other for more than a year are plottin' something?"

"Don't try to charm me, Wade Boudreaux. I know you and I know my husband. You two are up to something."

"All right, dawlin'," said Wade, with a clandestine wink to Pete; "you got us. But you gonna ruin your own surprise. Pete and I were plannin' to cook a good ol' Cajun dinner for you girls tonight. We were just gettin' ready to make groceries."

"Well, dat sounds great," said Molly, poking fun at Wade. "What do you think, Debbie?"

"Great. We can sit here and drink our beer while the boys make groceries."

"You guys and your expressions," smiled Molly. "Is making groceries a Cajun thing?"

"No Mol, that's more of a N'awlins thing," said Wade. "Most of the Cajun expressions have some French in them. Like *avoir un bobo* means to have a little injury and *make dodo* means to go to sleep. Most of the N'awlins sayings are just weird things like callin' the middle ground on a boulevard the neutral ground or yellin' 'Who dat?!' at a Saints game. I guess you gotta live there to appreciate it. OK, Pete, let's go. Piggly Wiggly or Winn Dixie?"

"Piggly Wiggly seems more appropriate," Pete said dryly.

Pete and Wade fetched fresh beers for the girls and collected Molly's grocery list before walking out to the car.

"So what are we cooking, Wade?"

"Hell if I know. We'll figure it out when we get there. I had to come up with something. Your wife's like a damn coon dog. You can't get anything past her."

"You got that right. I'm glad you thought of something, 'cause I was just sitting there looking stupid."

"Yeah, you good at that."

They drove Pete's Honda to the market, taking a detour by the Ferguson family cemetery. The two walked to the fence and opened the wooden gate. More than a century of Fergusons rested alongside Clay, who was buried under freshly turned soil. Someone had recently placed fresh flowers at Clay's and several other graves. Pete suspected it was Walter. Over the bluff, they could see a fishing boat motoring across the sound. The smell of the marsh and wet leaves hung in the air. Wade crossed himself as they walked through the gate.

"Since you're sticking your neck out for me and Clay Stevens, I thought you'd like to visit his grave."

"I wish I had known Clay. He made a big impact on you."

"That he did."

"You know, you can learn a lot about somebody goin' to the funeral or seein' the grave. I used to go to the grave sometimes when I was in the FBI."

"What can you tell about Clay?"

"Anybody who endeared himself to a family enough to earn a spot in the family plot must have been quite a man. I bet Clay was genuine and honest. An old slave family like the Fergusons is probably like my family and can spot a phony a mile away. Old families that stick together are good at that. Judgin' from the epitaph, he was a God-fearin' man. If he was wealthy, you wouldn't guess it from the headstone. It fits right in with the others."

"I think you've got him figured pretty well. You and Clay probably would have hit it off. Of course, with you never meeting a stranger, it's hard to believe that you couldn't get along with most folks."

"We didn't know each other when I was a N'awlins cop. I met quite a few men on the force that I could live without. We had as many criminals on the force as on the streets. Murder, bribery, extortion, racism, intimidation, brutality, theft, rape—you name it, and they were into it."

"Did you try to do something about it?"

"One, I ain't no Frank Serpico. I wasn't about to get buried in the bayou goin' on some one-man crusade to clean up the NOPD. I did poke my nose around internal affairs, but *pooyie*, them bastards were as bad as the others. That's when I decided to get out. Two, even if I was stupid enough to push to clean up the force, there wasn't enough good folks on the city council to take any action. They made the term corrupt politician redundant. Graft, political favoritism, vote buyin', and insider deals ruled the day. I still get a knot in my gut when I think about them bastards. Maybe that's why I want to help you with this. I hate to see a powerful and corrupt bastard like Bennett get away with murder."

"I'm glad you're with me on this, Wade. You're a good friend."

"You know, in N'awlins, we bury above ground."

"I guess I did know that. I'd like to visit a cemetery there sometime."

"They're interestin' places. They call 'em cities of the dead. In N'awlins, that whole family would be buried in one or two tombs," Wade pointed as they walked to the car. "Saves on space."

"Well you can't fit all those caskets in one tomb."

"Right. Those tombs get hot as an oven. Bodies decompose quickly. When the next one dies, they sweep up the ashes and put 'em in a sack in the bottom of the tomb. We take one of them cemetery tours the next time you come to visit."

Wade and Pete bought fixings for shrimp etouffée. Wade wanted crawfish, but when he asked for them, the lady at the seafood counter looked at him like he was from another planet. They found rice, vegetables, onions, fresh uncooked, unpeeled shrimp, and to Wade's surprise, cayenne pepper.

"This cayenne pepper will melt the chrome off a trailer hitch. I'll go easy on it for you virgins and add more to mine at the table."

"I appreciate that Wade. I'd hate to burn a hole in my stomach just before I commit my first felony."

"I can't believe how backward y'all are here not havin' any crawfish."

"Having someone from Louisiana call Carolina backward is a real insult. Y'all just got running water a few years ago, didn't you?"

"That's a good one, Pete. I'll be sure to put a fresh coat of paint on the seat in the outhouse before you come. I'd hate you to get a splinter in your butt."

CHAPTER 28

▼

Employees eager to start their weekend paid no attention to Walter's evening work schedule. At 9 p.m., he carried his tool bag and two radios to the administrative area. He thoroughly checked all the offices and conference rooms to be certain no employees remained. Walter watched the last of the visitors walk to their cars as he shut off the water supply to the drinking fountain, unplugged it, and slowly disassembled the water connection. He listened to Braves baseball on a small radio as he waited.

Pete and Wade left for Walter's at 8:30. There, they met Rick Dawson and all changed into coveralls from Wal-Mart. At Wade's insistence, all emptied their bladders before leaving. They drove in two cars to the church parking lot, leaving Pete's car backed up to the woods near the end of the rope. All three rode to the hospital in Rick's Mercedes, parking in the corner of the lot near the administrative building. They said little on the way. Wade had taken them through so many dry runs that any further discussion would only distract them. Second thoughts came to Pete as they sneaked along the edge of the parking lot. He wondered if they should have moved Molly and Debbie to a hotel for the night.

The three moved through shadows along the edge of the building and met Walter at the door. Thunder rumbled in the distance. Without a word, Walter gave a radio to Wade as they moved to Carver's office. Walter opened the door with his master key and returned to his position at the fountain. They tested the radios once. Wade closed the blinds and gave the OK to turn on the lights and shut the door. Rick sat at the computer, pushing the button to boot up the system. The computer hummed while the software came to life during what seemed like an eternity. Finally, a dialog box appeared on the screen signifying the need for a password.

"Shit, password required," lamented Rick.

"Don't worry. Put in this disk before you reboot."

Within minutes, Wade's disk allowed access into Carver's system.

"OK. Here's your disk back, Wade. Microsoft Windows. Here we go. He's got a bunch of documents in folders in Microsoft Word and a bunch of spread-sheets in Excel. The rest of this is Windows, some utility programs and a screen-saver. I'm just going to copy everything he's got in Word and in Excel, and we'll sort it out later. Look here. He's got a folder titled Stevens."

"Be sure to get that one, Rick. Also be sure to get anything that looks like it might be for the foundation," Wade said.

"Yeah, he's got a folder for the foundation in both programs."

While Rick switched diskettes in and out of the drive on the computer, Wade and Pete sorted through books.

"Accounting, tax law, directory of hospitals, a dictionary, medical staff bylaws. I'm not coming up with much here," Pete said. His worries left him as Pete con-centrated on his job. *This isn't so hard.*

"Me either. It's probably all on the computer. We need to keep looking."

The three jumped at the sound of the radio crackling to life.

"Two kids comin' into the area. Gimme a minute to get rid of them," Walter said in a low voice.

Wade shut off the light, locked the door, and the three sat still. Pete's heart pounded. He felt hot. *Maybe it's not so easy.* Wade rested like a cool Cajun cucumber.

"Can I help you, gents," Walter asked two unkempt boys who appeared to be 16 or 17. They were hospital visitors who took a wrong turn trying to leave the building.

"We just goin' out to our car, gramps."

"I'm sorry, but you can't get out this door at night, fellas. Let me show you the way back to the main entrance."

"Sure, Pops, whatever you say," said the one with the tattoo on his neck that looked like a dog collar.

Wade turned on the lights after Walt gave the OK. Within minutes, Wade picked the lock on the filing cabinet. He opened the top drawer of the credenza and sifted through the files.

"I don't know why they even put locks on these things. My cat could get this open. I'm findin' nothing of interest here, boys. There's got to be a safe in here. Pete, check behind those pictures on the wall."

"Rick, get up outa that chair."

Wade rolled the desk chair off to the side and lifted the plastic carpet protector off the floor. He dropped to his knees. Running his fingers through the carpet he found a recessed brass ring in the carpet in front of the desk. Pulling it opened a two by two-foot section of the sub-floor, revealing a small floor safe with a tumbler lock.

"Now we cookin'. This is an ol' safe. I should be able to crack it. Y'all be still now."

Wade pulled a small electronic instrument from his bag and stretched out flat on his belly. He attached an earpiece and slowly turned the dial.

As Wade worked, Pete searched the bottom drawer of the file.

"32—24—12," said Pete, with a big smile on his face.

"Shhhh," said an irritated Wade.

"Try 32—24—12."

"What in hell are you talkin' about?"

"I found the combination, Mr. Safecracker. These numbers are on a scrap of paper in the S file. If I'm right, this guy really is dimwitted. He may as well have just written them on the front of the safe."

Wade removed the earpiece and turned the dial to the requisite numbers. He then rotated the brass lever causing a familiar clunking and clicking sound. He opened the circular door to find 20-dollar bills tied in a roll with a rubber band and a stack of papers folded in half.

Gibby Morgan struggled to fix a running light on his boat. He wished he were at home with a beer in front of the baseball game. It was times like this, that Gibby thought his boat might be more trouble and expense than it was worth. Mosquitoes nagged him while he messed up the head of a screw trying to remove a part. When his radio squawked, he banged his head.

"Shit." He held a greasy rag against the top of his head.

"Dispatch to Sheriff Morgan."

"Morgan, go ahead, dispatch."

"I'm getting a silent alarm from the administration area at the hospital. Code book says call you first. You want me to send a unit?"

"No, I'll check it out." *This is the last damn thing I need right now. It's probably the weather.* He removed his revolver from the glove box and headed to the hospital.

"*Sacre!*" cried Wade, as he rose to his feet. "We hit the mother lode. Look here, Rick. These look like ledgers to me. Dates up and down and names goin' across. These numbers gotta be payments."

"There seem to be four sets here," said Rick.

"Be careful to keep 'em in order," warned Wade.

"Look, this set has ECEP at the top. Two thousand bucks a month to Bennett. It stopped a few months ago. What in hell does ECEP stand for?"

"That's an easy one," said Pete. "East Coast Emergency Physicians. They were the group who had the ER contract before me. No wonder they were paying so poorly with Bennett sucking off 2K a month. The owner of that group must have been making a killing if he could toss $2,000 a month in pay-offs. What a dirt bag. What else is there?" Pete would enjoy exposing the owner of the group and watching the docs jump ship. Another parasite off the butt of emergency medicine.

"The next stack is the foundation. This is a lot more complicated. It looks like Bennett is in on this, too. The numbers vary, but he averages about 1500 a month. L.C. is the other column. This must be our boy, Carver. He's doing about the same. I'll have to review the stuff on the computer to figure out how they're skimming off the foundation. The next stack is the hospital. There are four columns—MB for Bennett, LC for Carver, GM, and ED. Now we're starting to see some real money. Bennett is getting six or seven grand a month—1,000 a month for Carver and for ED, and 500 for GM. They're probably doing this with dummy vendors and corporations. Hopefully, I'll find a spreadsheet on that. So who are GM and ED?"

"I don't know," said Pete.

"Don't look at me," said Wade.

"Now here's the interesting pile," said Rick. "These say LAB at the top."

"I'll put down money it's Betts' lab," offered Pete.

"That's my guess, too," said Rick. "OK, we've got four columns. This is where the real action is. Damn. Fifteen or 20 grand a month. WB must be Wilhelm Betts. MB is Bennett. LC is Carver. Then there's DC. I'm stumped on that one. What do you guys think?"

"I'll have to think about that one," said Pete.

"I don't know about initials but I do know that we're pushin' our luck stayin' in here any longer," said Wade. I'm goin' to make copies of this, and then we'll get the hell out."

With papers in hand, Wade walked to the copy room at the end of the far hallway. He closed the door and went to work. Because the papers were folded and wrinkled he did not risk tearing them by using the automatic feeder. Rick and Pete carefully put things back in their place in Carver's office. Rick shut down the computer and stuck the disk in his pocket.

"Who's down here with you, Walter?" asked Gibby Morgan, as Walt tightened the nut on the fountain.

Time and Walter's heart stopped momentarily. Gibby Morgan seemed to come out of nowhere. There was no way to warn the others. He would just have to wing it.

"Hey, Gibby. What you been up to?" said Walt, speaking loudly enough to be heard in Carver's office but not enough to be heard in the copy room.

Rick and Pete turned off the light, locked the door, and sat silently on the floor.

"Not much, Walt. Is anybody else down here?"

"I don't know, Gibby. I'm not really payin' attention. I'm just tryin' to fix this fountain before I go home for the weekend. I'm pretty sure that everybody's been gone for hours."

"I'm just going to take a look around."

The silent alarm came from the trap door in Carver's office. Wade failed to see the switch to disengage the alarm prior to opening the safe door. There had been false alarms due to weather and electrical surges in the past. Gibby was more suspicious than usual because of his recent meeting with Carver. He walked through the halls, checking doors to offices and meeting rooms. Most were locked and those that were unlocked were empty. He continued past Carver's office after finding the door secured.

"Walt. Everything OK?" Wade called on the radio.

"Did you say something, Walt?" asked Gibby with a perplexed look on his face.

"No, it must be the game on the radio you heard."

Before Walt could turn down the volume on the radio Wade repeated himself.

"Walt, that's not the game. Who's on the other radio, friend?" asked Gibby, in a more suspicious tone.

"Oh, him. I've got a new assistant. He's down in the shop finishin' up some work on a mower while I fix this. He's a good kid. I think he's just worried about me being up here by myself. I told him about my heart condition."

"I'm OK. I'll be down to help you finish up with the mower in a few minutes," Walter lied into the radio.

It was too late. Gibby could hear the transmission come out of the other radio as Wade moved toward them. Gibby moved toward the sound and began to unbuckle his service revolver.

"Walt, you better not move a muscle. I don't know what you're up to—"

Gibby Morgan and Wade Boudreaux came within an arm's length of each other as they met at the corner. Wade had already drawn his .38 when Walt failed to respond to the radio the first time.

"Don't do it," Wade commanded, as Gibby held his hand at the holster. "Interlace your fingers behind your head."

"I'm a cop. I'm not gonna do that," said Gibby with conviction.

"I used to be a cop too, so I know how you feel. You do what I say or I'll shoot you in the damn foot," responded Wade more convincingly.

"All right. You're in a heap of shit, pal. Why don't you give me that gun now before things get any worse," said Gibby, as he followed Wade's command.

Rick and Pete sat in the dark in disbelief. Both felt helpless. There was nothing to do but sit and wait while Wade committed aggravated assault.

"Walt, come remove this gentleman's side arm from the holster for me. We're goin' to move to this conference room so we can't be seen."

As they began to move to the conference room, Wade felt cold steel on the back of his neck.

"Drop it or you're a quadriplegic," shouted Larry Carver.

Carver heard the voices as he entered the administrative area. He had slipped down the far hallway and approached from behind. He, too, was suspicious and decided to respond to the alarm when notified by the dispatcher. From the conversation on the other side of the door, Rick concluded that things were not going well. He removed the disk from his pocket and placed it deep in the wood chips that surrounded the stem of a fake ficus tree in Carver's office.

"Shit. OK. I'm gonna lower my weapon," said a dejected Wade.

"Walter, I can't believe you're tied up in this," said Gibby, as he turned to retrieve his weapon. "What in hell are you two doing?"

"Don't say anything, Walt," advised Wade.

"Shut the hell up, asshole," said Carver, as he relieved Wade of his weapon.

Gibby frisked Walter and Wade, finding no other weapons. He gave Carver the papers Wade had stuffed in his jacket. The four moved into the conference room. Walter and Wade sat in chairs at the end of the table while Carver and Morgan stood at the head.

"You have no idea what you've gotten yourselves into," Carver said anxiously, as he examined the ledger sheets.

"We've got a pretty good idea," Wade said calmly.

"Who are you and how did you get this far?" barked Carver, pointing at Wade.

Wade sat in silence and gave a reassuring nod to Walter. Gibby and Carver stepped into the hall.

"Gibby, eventually they'll figure out these ledgers. We have no choice. If we fail to protect him, the goddamn world will come down on us. We can't risk it," said Carver.

"You're right. This is clean so far. We can sweep up and get out of here without leaving a trace. Let's take our time and do this right with no mistakes. Check out your office and get it back in order. I'll sit with these two."

Carver unlocked his office to find Pete and Rick sitting on the floor leaning against his desk. The two looked like teenagers waiting in the vice principal's office after being caught smoking in the bathroom.

"What the hell? Who else is in on this, the damn housekeeper? You two come with me. Fredericks, we should have done you after we missed the first time." He walked Rick and Pete to the conference room and carried a bag they were holding. "Gibby, I found two more in my office."

Pete wondered how they would get out of this, and how he would explain their actions. This was no prank. He figured his job was lost for sure, and poor Walt was gonna get fired and probably lose his pension.

"Well, bring 'em in here and I'll frisk 'em," said Gibby. "Doc, I'm sorry to see you in on this. You're in way over your head, son."

"I can say the same for you, Gibby. Sorry sack of shit," said Pete, as he realized the identity of GM.

Carver closed the safe and pocketed the cash left sitting on his desk. He returned the carpet protector and the chair to the proper location. While his computer booted up, he looked around the office. He failed to notice the small bits of wood chips next to his artificial tree, which had been disturbed by Dawson. Using Windows, he copied any sensitive files to disk and then deleted them from his hard drive. He opened Norton Utilities and ran a government sweep of the hard drive to remove any last remnants of the files. He shredded the originals and copies of the ledgers before returning to the conference room.

"You find any computer disks, Gibby?"

"Yeah, the bag had a box of unmarked disks and mystery man here had one marked 'Boot'."

"It doesn't matter now if they got in my system or not. We'll destroy the disks after we get rid of these four troublemakers. How do you want to do it?" asked Carver.

"I been thinkin' about that," said Gibby.

CHAPTER 29

▼

Once Gibby Morgan and Larry Carver returned the administrative area to normal, they escorted the four felons to Rick's Mercedes. Gibby had tied their hands behind their backs with the duct tape they had purchased at Wal-Mart and gagged them with pieces of towel. The four prisoners crammed themselves into the back seat. Carver drove to the marina as Gibby watched the others at gunpoint. They parked at the back of the marina building. Gibby left the others behind while he searched the area. Carver walked the prisoners to a picnic table and helped them sit down.

"Just sit here for a minute while I do a couple of things," Gibby said.

He started the Mercedes and pulled it to the top of the long boat ramp. He secured the steering wheel with a length of rope and made sure the wheels were straight. Leaving the car in gear, he applied the parking brake and rolled down the driver's side window. Gibby stepped out, closed the door, and reached in the window to release the parking brake. Rick closed his eyes as the others watched the sedan slip into the waterway. A sound reminiscent of a single ocean wave penetrated the still night air as Rick's beloved motorcar entered the black water. Bubbles would rise for another 15 minutes. Pete wondered how close the car landed to the engine from Clay's skiff.

Gibby started the engines of his 30-foot twin-engine fishing boat. Many on Hilton Head wondered how a man making $50,000 a year could afford a boat that cost at least that much. Most figured that he inherited money. As the Yamaha Saltwater Series 200-horse engines came to life, Gibby motioned for Carver to bring the four desperadoes to the boat. Walking single file down the pier with arms secured behind their backs and mouths gagged, Pete began to consider his mortality. Gibby steadied them as each stepped down onto the back deck of the boat. He instructed them to sit on the deck by the stern as he handed Carver an empty plastic bag.

"Collect some empty beer cans from the trash over there."

"For what?" asked Carver, with a perplexed look on his face.

"You'll see. Just do it."

Gibby pulled a bottle of Scotch whiskey and a shot glass from a storage bin under the console. He took a long swig from the bottle, then wiped his mouth on his sleeve.

"Listen, shitheads. You're each gonna drink four shots of this and you're not gonna give me any grief about it."

Wade elbowed Pete on one side and Rick on the other. He emphatically shook his head back and forth.

"Enough of that," shouted Gibby. "You're gonna do this or I'm gonna pistol whip the crap out of you."

One at a time, Gibby untied the gags while each man downed his required amount of whiskey. Carver returned with a dozen empty cans of various types of beer as Gibby replaced the last gag. Alcohol was alcohol—beer or whiskey. Carver cast off the mooring lines as Gibby headed the boat to the north end of the island.

"I thought we were going out to sea?" asked Carver.

"In time. These boys are gonna have a little accident. We need Ferguson's boat to make it look convincing."

Gibby piloted his fishing boat slowly and quietly up the waterway creating little wake. A full moon and clear skies made navigation easy for Gibby who had memorized the locations of the green and red markers of the waterway. Gibby and Carver spoke little. The four prisoners sat with heads hung. For Pete, the alcohol heightened the surreal experience of being taken to one's death. Wade gave up attempting to release his wrists from the duct tape. The twisting motion served only to tighten the tape and cause his hands to go numb.

Gibby slowed the boat as he steered into the inlet behind Walter's house. Even at springtide, the boat barely floated in the shallow inlet. Gibby tilted the engines enough to prevent damage to his propellers but not enough to cause noisy cavitation. They found Walter's 10-foot wooden rowboat with 15-horse outboard engine tied to the pier. It still smelled of a fresh coat of hunter green marine paint that Walter applied the previous weekend. Carver walked to the bow and untied the boat. Having limited room to turn, Gibby chose to back out while Carver held the line to the rowboat.

Once in the waterway, Carver walked the rowboat to the stern, tying it to a cleat. Carver now understood the *accident* that Gibby planned for their captives. The trip to the mouth of the waterway took 30 minutes. Once beyond earshot of anyone who could identify his craft, Gibby accelerated to 25 mph. In tow, the rowboat shifted back and forth between sides of the wake until he stopped three miles offshore. Gibby pulled the rowboat along side his boat and dumped the beer cans into the rowboat. The clatter startled Walter, who had drifted off to sleep because of the alcohol and the droning sound of the engines. Gibby leaned over the gunwale of his boat as he pushed the gunwale of Walter's rowboat under the cold ocean water, allowing it to fill three quarters of the way. Tethered by the rubber hose running to the engine, the gasoline tank floated as the beer cans scattered inside. Gibby knew the calm ocean would help preserve the accident scene. He cast off the rowboat and returned to the console. He took another swig of whiskey before speeding another half mile off shore.

Gibby never expected that his involvement with Morton Bennett, Carver, and Betts would lead to committing not one murder but five. Even in his duties as sheriff, he had never killed anyone. Self-preservation outweighed any reservations about the crime he was about to perpetrate. Gibby knew he would be eliminated before the next high tide if he crossed these men. This had been expressed to him subtly by Dick Coswell on several occasions.

"Let's get this over with," Gibby said with resignation. "Remove their gags and take the tape off their wrists. Don't any of you assholes get smart. I'll just shoot you and we'll sink your bodies another five miles off shore. Larry, soak a rag with some gas to get the glue from the tape off their wrists."

"Walt, I'm sorry friend," said Pete, feeling guilty.

"It's not your fault, Pete. We all knew there might be trouble. I got no regrets. We're in the Lord's hands—grace will lead us home."

"Shut up, you two," Larry barked.

"All right. Everybody in the drink," said Gibby.

"I wanna ask you one question before I go in," said Wade. "Who is D.C.?"

"Let's just say he and his boss are gonna be in the White House next election," boasted Gibby. Now in ya go."

It was then that Pete realized that DC was Coswell and ED was Buddy. He remembered Buddy's given name was Emerson. One at a time, they jumped into the 55-degree ocean.

As Gibby approached the no wake zone, he slowed the engines and pulled his cell phone from his pocket.

"Red line."

"Dick, it's Gibby. Carver and I interrupted a burglary of his office at the hospital. We cleaned the site and have just disposed of the burglars. It's gonna look like a fishing accident. The burglary was an amateur job by some locals. Everything is under control now. All sensitive information has been destroyed."

"Well done. Triple check to make sure you've got all the bases covered. I want to hear right away if things heat up."

CHAPTER 30

▼

Pete, Walt, Wade, and Rick treaded water and shivered in the black water of the Atlantic. They may as well have been a thousand miles off shore. There was enough light from the moon to see the fear in each other's eyes, but not enough to know the direction back to Hilton Head. Pete thought about swimming back to the island, but for all he knew they'd be swimming to Bermuda. He also worried about Walt's heart and wondered how long his friend could hold out.

"Everybody get your shoes off," Pete said, trying to seem calm. He felt anything but calm. "Unlace your shoes and hang onto the laces." Three minutes in the water and fingers and toes felt like they belonged to someone else. Anxiety about drowning and the dense cold made breathing a chore. "Coveralls off next and hang on to them." Pete knew there were sharks around the island. Nobody at the beach ever got bitten. They weren't at the beach. "Tie each leg off with a lace—tight now." His speech quickened and the tone rose higher with each command. "What you gotta do is hold at the waist and swing them over your head to catch air. Then you gotta cross the arms and roll the torso down to seal the air in." They each tried a couple of times until it worked. The pants looked like scarecrow legs filled with air, but it kept them afloat.

"Damn, you smarter than I thought," Wade said breathlessly. "Where'd you learn this?"

"Boy Scout motto is 'Be Prepared'," Pete said. He remembered when he learned it, he thought he'd never have to use it. "You OK, Walt?"

"Yeah, how 'bout you?"

"I'm OK."

"That's fantastic," Walt responded, in his most enthusiastic voice. "Wade?"

"I'm great."

"Awesome," Walt yelled. "Dawson?"

"I am superb," Rick yelled back.

"Anybody drunk?" Walt yelled.

"Hell no," the other three yelled back.

"Good, I knew you boys could hold your liquor."

Pete caught on to what Walt was doing. Stay upbeat. Keep the emotional energy high. "We're gonna get through this," Pete said with determination.

"Damn straight," Walt said.

"You're gonna have to fill your coveralls with air every few minutes," Pete said, feeling better after Walt's cheerleading. Try to conserve your energy. We gotta put our heads together now. Anybody got an idea?"

No sound. No wind. No waves. No trees rustling. No bugs or frogs. Complete silence.

"I don't have an idea, but hearing no sound is freaking me out," Pete said with half a laugh. "Come on Walt, you grew up here."

"Sandbars. I always warned Clay about goin' off shore. There are some real shallow spots at low tide. I don't know if they're out this far. I actually never been out this far."

"When's the next low tide?" Pete said.

"I'm guessin' four hours—give or take an hour," Walt said, as he readied to refill his coveralls.

"Sounds good, Walt, but how we gonna find a sand bar?" Wade said.

"I'm just thinkin' out loud, fellas. I haven't gotten that far yet."

They treaded in silence for another minute. Even with the makeshift floatation, Pete was feeling fatigued. His legs cramped and all skin below water was numb. He wondered if he'd ever find his testicles again. Pete knew they would have to start moving or they would all die of hypothermia. The other three were looking lethargic.

"We'll swim toward the moon," Pete said, out of breath. "That way, we don't swim in circles. Maybe we'll come across a shallow spot." A wave of fear came over him as he watched Walt float onto his back.

"Walt."

No answer.

"His ears are under water," Rick said.

"Walt!" Pete yelled. Walt lifted his head. "You OK?"

"I'm having some chest pain. I thought it would be easier if I floated on my back."

"All right, you tell me when it passes and we'll start swimming."

CHAPTER 31

▼

After hanging up with Gibby, Coswell decided it was time for damage control and time to quit the Hilton Head operation while they were still ahead.

"Wilhelm, it's Dick."

"Yes, Dick." Betts answered groggily. "How are you?"

"Not good. It's time to cut and run—just like we planned if things get out of hand."

"What is happening?" Betts said, as he sat on the edge of the bed and pushed his hair back over his forehead.

Coswell went on to explain the events of the evening. He reminded Betts of the long-standing emergency plan to dismantle his lab and move any inventory onto his yacht to make a quick departure to Bermuda.

"Dick, are you sure of this thing? Huge inventory of OxyContin we have right now. Very smooth our process is now. Never before do we make so much."

"Yes, I'm sure," Coswell said forcefully. "We have no choice. I have a crew on the way to eliminate anyone who knows about this but you and your lab crew. Get your crew out of bed. Dismantle the lab and move your inventory to the yacht. You need to be motoring east by noon. You knew it would come to this some day."

"Yes, Dick. This I know. I do what you say. I call you when we leave."

CHAPTER 32

▼

Saturday morning, Molly and Debbie awoke to find that their husbands had not returned from the card game they said they went to at Walter's. Debbie assumed that the men were too drunk to walk and decided to sleep there. They walked to Walter's, planning to roust them out of bed, but found all the doors at Walter's locked. There were no cars and no signs of life. Growing more worried, Molly and Debbie walked back home. They called the hospital, the marina, the club, and finally the police. A deputy arrived within minutes. Molly and Debbie greeted Deputy Jack Gurba on the front porch.

"Wade Boudreaux and my husband went to play cards down the road at Walter Ferguson's last night. They never returned. We have checked everywhere they might be, and there is no sign of them. These are two responsible men. It is very unlike them to be away for so long without at least checking in."

"I'm sorry to hear about your troubles, Mrs. Fredericks. I know your husband from the hospital. He treated me when I had a concussion."

"Oh, yes," said Molly. "I remember Pete telling me about that."

"Why don't you ladies sit down in these chairs so I can gather some information? Did your husbands have plans to do anything else last night besides play cards at Mr. Ferguson's?"

"No," Molly said.

"What about today? Any plans?"

"No," Debbie said, in a strained voice.

"You and your husband are just here to visit?"

"Yes, we've been right here most of the week except for a trip to Savannah. We're going to see Dr. Betts next week."

"What kind of work does your husband do?"

"He's retired from the FBI. Now he's a private investigator."

"Did he have any business on the island or could something have followed him here from a case at home?"

"As far as I know, I don't think so. He doesn't tell me about every case, but I don't think he had anything big going. He's never done any work here on the island. This is our first visit here."

Gurba explained that someone would need to be missing more than 24 hours for the sheriff's office to devote much effort to finding him. The deputy reassured them that this is a common occurrence on Saturday mornings and that people usually turn up by noon. He gathered photos and information about Pete's vehicle and promised to take a look around while on patrol. A detective would be assigned the case if the two did not return by the next morning.

Molly decided she needed to push things along. She convinced Debbie that it would be best if she stayed behind so one of them was there if the men showed up. Molly headed to the home of the only person who could speed up a search for the men—Gibby Morgan.

CHAPTER 33

▼

The weather was partly cloudy and a pleasant 65 degrees that morning. A shrimp boat with a crew of two headed south on the Intracoastal Waterway, appearing to prepare for a day of harvesting shrimp. Large booms with green netting protruded like big flagpoles from the sides of the weathered boat, which badly needed a coat of white paint. Miss Barbara was lettered across each side of the bow. The low-pitched hum of the diesel engine rolled across the waterway as the crew prepared for the day. Each wore the traditional white rubber shrimp boots and yellow waterproof overalls. The captain's ruddy face and neck attested to years of hard work in the wind and sun. The younger man wore a baseball cap with a Skoal chewing tobacco patch sewn on it. He was tall, slim, and clean cut, with buzz-cut black hair.

The captain slowed the engine as the boat neared the estate of Morton Bennett. The younger man turned his cap backwards as he entered the small musty boat cabin. He opened a padded plastic case containing a hunting rifle equipped with a high-powered sight and a silencer. After opening the cabin window, he raised binoculars to his eyes and located Morton Bennett, who was sitting on his wooden deck and reading the morning paper. The shrimper approached unnoticed by Bennett. Resting the rifle on the windowsill, the younger man found Bennett in the gun site. The lack of wind and waves made his job all the easier. He slowly lifted the barrel off the sill and steadied the rifle. As he took a deep breath, he confirmed his aim, and squeezed the trigger. The muffled sound of the rifle was lost in the sound of the engine. Not even the skipper heard it. Before the killer exhaled, the bullet pierced the skull of Morton Bennett above the left eye, causing a painless and instant death. Bennett slumped in the chair as if sleeping.

The killer had been instructed to eliminate Tami Bennett if possible; otherwise, another man would assume the duty. He could see a woman who was
standing in the kitchen behind a large picture window but could not be assured
of a kill through the glass. A miss would be worse than doing nothing. As he
pulled the rifle back from the window, Tami Bennett stepped onto the deck, carrying a pot of coffee. The killer quickly found her in his site. Tami bent over to
pour coffee, not realizing her brother's fate. As she stood up, a bullet ripped into
her chest. Her death was rapid but not painless. She collapsed to the ground as
the coffeepot shattered on the deck. She breathlessly made a weak cry for help as
her thorax filled with blood. Within two minutes she lay unconscious, and within
five minutes was dead. The killer returned his weapon to the case as the shrimper
headed to the Atlantic. Before exiting the cabin, the younger man pulled a cell
phone from his overalls. He speed dialed to another secure cell phone.

"Mama Bear and Papa Bear are down."

Within two minutes, an eight-foot inflatable outboard boat skimmed up onto
the narrow beach of the Bennett estate. The 25-year-old driver wore blue nylon
shorts, a tan T-shirt, a Boston Red Sox cap, sunglasses, and rubber beach shoes.
He was short and sturdy with shoulder-length sandy hair. Jumping over the edge
of the boat, he threw a small backpack over his shoulder. He calmly walked to the
sea wall and took the steep winding stairs up to the deck. The privacy the Bennetts enjoyed helped the killers to complete their work without detection. The
young man quickly confirmed the two deaths by checking each body for a carotid
pulse, slipped on white gloves, and entered the home. Knowing exactly where to
go, he entered the office to find that the computer was running. He shut the
blinds, unplugged the computer and quickly removed the cover to the CPU.
Within three minutes, the hard drive was in his backpack and back-up disks had
been located. He removed a wallet from the top desk drawer, then quickly moved
to the bedrooms. There he found a fortune in jewelry, which he added to the
backpack. A gold Rolex, several sets of diamond earrings and matching necklaces,
a pearl necklace, and several gold bracelets were easily found. A search through
dresser drawers yielded an exquisite necklace, wrapped in a black felt cloth, set
with at least 30 diamonds. He exited, removed his gloves, and calmly took the
steps back to the boat. The departure was more difficult than the landing because
of the deep, sticky mud five yards off the beach. He plodded through the mud,
pulling the boat off the beach until it floated. After climbing back into the craft,
he rowed to deeper water so he could start the engine, and then sped to a rendez-
vous with the shrimper.

The smaller craft caught up to the shrimp boat as it neared the south end of the island. After boarding the shrimper, he and the other gunman changed into clean running shoes, black cargo pants, and T-shirts with Island Environmental Tours and a sea turtle logo on the front. They donned dark sunglasses and caps that matched the shirts. The cargo pants were equipped with semi-automatic handguns in the large side pockets. Other pockets held hunting knives, ropes, cellular phones, and one of those all-in-one folding tools that looks like a pliers. The taller man dialed Gibby Morgan's home. Still sleeping because of his nocturnal activities, Gibby answered on the fifth ring. Carver, who was sleeping on the couch, stirred also.

"Hello," said Gibby in a groggy voice.

"Gibby Morgan?"

"Yeah, who's calling?"

"Please stay where you are. Expect a call from the senator soon."

"Hello?" said a bewildered Gibby into an empty line.

Molly paid five dollars to get through the gate at Sea Pines Plantation. That five dollars burned her every time she paid it. She took Cordillo Parkway and turned right on North Sea Pines Drive. She strained to find the sign for Sandhill Crane Road, then turned left. Having been divorced three years before, Gibby lived alone. This fact was not difficult to discern from the street because of the neglected landscaping, mundane window treatments, and lack of flowers in the yard. The home, and Gibby, clearly lacked a woman's touch. Loud voices filtered from inside as Molly approached.

"Duke is calling?" Carver fumed. "We're screwed."

"Why do you say that?" Gibby said defensively.

"Did you ever talk to him directly before?"

"No, always Coswell," Gibby said perplexed.

"Well, he's not calling to make you chairman of his campaign," Carver barked. I'm getting off this island until things cool down." Carver walked to the door and opened it part way.

"Larry, we'll never get nailed for drownin' those four."

Molly could hear the conversation through the door. Tears welled in her eyes as she stood frozen on the front steps of Gibby's house.

"That may be so," Carver said, looking back at Gibby as he nearly walked into Molly, "but Duke sure knows something's up."

When Carver's eyes met Molly's, she turned to run. Gibby did not recognize her, but Carver did. He had met Molly at a hospital function. She sprinted across the yard, dodging azalea bushes and palmetto trees. She would have made it but for tripping over a pine tree stump. She tumbled into a row of crepe myrtle. Looking like the before pictures for a diet pill ad, Carver and Gibby barreled toward Molly. She tried to kick and scream but Carver and Gibby wrangled her and covered her mouth before any of the neighbors could hear. Out of breath, they hauled Molly into the house, tied her wrists and ankles, and gagged her.

"Now what?" Carver gasped.

"Shit, this is gettin' out of control," Gibby fumed. "You gotta take her to Betts' place. Who knows what's gonna happen here with Duke callin'?"

The tall man and the short man boarded the inflatable boat and cast off from the shrimper. They sped around the southern tip of the island on smooth seas. It was early enough in the morning that the ocean waves and breeze had not yet stirred. The two men had met in military prison. Both served time for striking a superior officer. After their release and dishonorable discharge, they became proficient at the art of eliminating special problems for the rich and powerful. Their clients never learned their names or met them in person. Half the fee was paid in advance to a numbered offshore account. The other half was paid to a separate account upon completion of the job. This job earned them $50,000 per kill.

Finding a water tower landmark, they accelerated to the shore and beached the small craft. They would not be gone long enough to worry about the rising tide. Both calmly walked to the dune, taking a narrow footpath over it near an empty beach house. Upon reaching the street, they jogged four blocks inland to the two-bedroom home of Gibby Morgan.

The tall man rang the doorbell. Gibby, completely disconcerted, greeted them wearing sweatpants and a dull white muscle-man undershirt. Gibby's severe hangover was compounded by feelings of great remorse over the murders he had just perpetrated. With all self-esteem lost, he looked and felt like hell.

"What can I do for you fellas," said Gibby, in a low monotone voice.

"Are you Sheriff Gibby Morgan?" said the tall man in a bright voice.

"Yeah. Who's askin'?"

"We're sorry to bother you. I'm John Cobb and this is Bill Siegel," the tall man lied. "The senator has asked that you help us with a problem we have. Could we come inside and discuss it?"

"Yeah. I'm expecting a call from him. I suppose it will be about you two."

"I think you're right," said the short man. "He told us he would be calling you this morning."

As they entered Gibby's living room, the short man closed the door. The two drew their weapons, pointing them at Gibby. Too sleepy and hung over to fight, Gibby stood frozen. His heart raced, his eyes dilated, and sweat formed on his brow.

"What in hell is this?" asked a stunned Gibby, not enjoying having a weapon pointed at him for the second time in 24 hours.

"Just cooperate and everything will be fine," said the tall man. "Drop to your knees and lay on your back."

Gibby reluctantly eased himself down onto the ground. It didn't take long for him to realize his fate. As he lowered to his knees and then his back, he experienced an epiphany, understanding much too late that he had chosen poorly about many things in life. He was a bad husband, an overbearing father, a drunk, and a corrupt public official who had sold out his integrity. His bankrupt life was about to end, and he felt only ambivalence.

"Don't move now," the short man said.

The tall man stood above him ready to fire if necessary. The short man stood behind Gibby's head out of his line of vision. He pulled a plastic medicine bottle with a measuring dropper in the cap out of one of his pockets. He squeezed the rubber top to draw five cc's of potassium cyanide into the dropper. Simultaneously, they moved to restrain him. The tall man sat on Gibby's pelvis and held his arms. The short man kneeled down over him, holding Gibby's head between his knees. Gibby barely struggled. As he opened his mouth to yell, the short man squirted the cyanide into the back of his mouth, then pulled his jaw closed, being careful not to cause bruising. It didn't matter if Gibby swallowed. The cyanide absorbed quickly. His breathing quickened and he became agitated for several minutes. A generalized seizure lasted two minutes; he pissed himself and died.

The two men left Gibby on the floor with the bottle at his side. They touched his fingertips to the bottle and the dropper. The tall man wiped prints from the doorknob and then locked the front door. They returned their weapons to their cargo pants and exited through the side door, which locked as they closed it. They scurried through bushes onto an empty side street, and then jogged back to the beach.

Gibby Morgan had just committed suicide. Whether his suicide was tied to the murder of the others did not matter. All that mattered was that Gibby had been silenced. Three down, one to go.

As Carver pulled into an empty spot in Betts' four-car garage, Betts and his crew loaded his essential belongings into a large white van. Bags and boxes had been tossed haphazardly on top of dozens of boxes of OxyContin. Carver explained how he came to hold hostage the wife of a man he just killed only hours before.

"This thing is not so bad," Betts said. "Having hostage will give insurance for trip to Bermuda. Put her in van. We take her on yacht and when she is no longer needed, she go in ocean like her husband."

CHAPTER 34

▼

A 38-foot fishing boat sped along the Intracoastal Waterway, failing to slow for No Wake zones. Several homeowners shook their fists as the craft cruised by, creating a rather large wake. The captain ignored the homeowners' protests as his crew of three fishing buddies tended to the four men they had plucked from the sea that morning. The captain had left the marina the previous day for an offshore fishing expedition. They planned to spend most of the weekend at sea; however, a fierce storm 20 miles east forced them to return early. They never expected to find four men in underwear who were close to drowning.

"You fellas wanna tell us how you came to be swimming almost four miles off shore?" said one of the crew.

"It's a complicated story, men," explained Wade. It would be better off for y'all and us if you don't know how we got there. I'm sure it will all be in the papers tomorrow. Right now, the less y'all know, the better. All I can tell you is that we discovered some important people on this island have been stealin' money. They got us before we could get them."

"Where are you from?" asked another crewmember. "I ain't never heard no one talk like that."

"I was raised in southwest Louisiana. I live in N'awlin's now."

Pete chuckled to himself about the absurdity of the conversation as the two linguists discussed fishing in south Louisiana. He and the others were still cold and numb. They all wrapped in blankets, but no one could stop shivering. Pete warmed as he drank a cup of coffee. The euphoria of being saved began to fade and the reality of eluding the police settled. They needed to formulate a plan to recover the disk from Carver's office and report their attempted murder to an uncorrupted law enforcement agency. Wade and Rick went topside to sweet talk the captain into keeping quiet. Worried about Walter and his heart condition, Pete added another blanket to his friend.

For the first time since going into the water, Pete thought about what Gibby said about the initials DC and his boss going to the White House. He couldn't make himself believe that his good friend would be involved in such a mess or would authorize the murders. To accept this as fact would require him to mourn the loss of one of his most trusted friends. Buddy may as well have been dead.

"Thanks," Walt said, as he patted Pete's leg.

"Don't worry about it. You look cold," Pete said, settling in next to Walt.

"No, I mean thanks for bein' my friend."

"We went through quite a scrape there, huh?"

"Close as they come, I guess."

"Molly's not gonna forgive me for this."

"She'll forgive you. But you gotta ask," Walt said, as he tightened his blankets around his shoulders. "God gives us a big capacity to forgive. I know it's in her. You gonna forgive yourself?"

"Yeah, sure," Pete said as he turned toward Walt.

"What about the Flick case?"

"Molly told you about the Flick case?"

"You talk about a lot of things renovatin' a house with someone."

"So what do you want to know about it?"

"Do you think about it much?"

"It's over. I can't do anything to change what happened," Pete said, as he stood to refill their coffee cups. "I think about it every day. I wake up at 2 a.m. and it's in my head. I can't make it go away."

"You're right. Ya can't turn back time. And ya can't stop every bad thing from happenin'."

"I still keep thinking there was something I could have done," Pete said, looking down at his feet.

"And you can't forgive yourself." Walt paused until they made eye contact again. "As I hear it, there's nothing to forgive. But if you think there is, then you gotta forgive yourself."

"Easier said than done," Pete said, as he peered out the tiny window at the passing shoreline.

"These things never are. Nothin' about your work is easy. If it was, then I'd be doin' it, wouldn't I? You need to look at this from the outside in. Nobody is perfect. You can't make a man who is blind with rage lie down like a lamb. You don't make deaf people hear or lame old men get up and dance. That's not your department. That's God's business. God forgives you. Now it's your turn," Walt turned to look directly at Pete. "Here's what I know. We just passed through Calibogue Sound, right?"

"Yeah?"

"It's a deep sound. Calibogue is an Indian word that means deep spring. God, like that sound, is a deep spring of forgiveness. Drink from that spring, Pete. You'll never thirst again."

Rick stepped down into the cabin looking a bit warmer. Wade followed and refilled his cup of coffee.

"What's next, Pete?" Rick said.

"You and Walt have done more than your share. I think that it would be best if we took the two of you back to your place. Get Walt warmed up and see how he feels. If he doesn't perk up, you'll need to take him to the hospital. I'd like to avoid anyone knowing we're alive for as long as possible, so stay out of sight."

"That sounds good to me," Rick said. "I've got to let Rudy out anyway. He's probably had to pee since 6 a.m."

"Are you having any chest pain?" Pete asked.

"No, I'm just cold. As soon as I warm up, I'll be fine," said Walt.

"What do you think, Wade?" Pete said.

"Rick, I want you to call Molly and Debbie and tell them we're sorry for makin' them worry. Don't tell them any details. Just tell them we all right, and we be home soon. Tell 'em to stay home and not open the door for nobody—especially the police. "Pete, we need to get back to your car. You got a phone in there?"

"Yeah, what then?"

"First, we need to contact somebody in the Charleston office of the FBI. We can't risk goin' through the local cops. For all we know, they're all dirty. Then we gonna find old Mr. Larry Carver."

"Our other clothes are in my trunk. We can change when we get there."

"You got your keys?" said Wade."

"No. Gibby took them, but I'm one step ahead of you, pal. I keep an extra key in one of those magnetic boxes stuck to the front axle support."

"Talk about luck," said Rick.

"Hey, there's no luck to it," said Pete indignantly. "Be Prepared."

"OK, I'm convinced," said Rick.

"We be prepared all right," said Wade, wryly. "I left an extra .38 pistol in the trunk."

As the boat approached the marina, Wade convinced one of the fishermen to take Pete and him to the church behind the hospital and take Walter and Rick home. The few boat owners who were doing repairs paid little mind to the four men draped in blankets who were scurrying across the parking lot. The fisherman turned the heat on high for his shivering passengers.

"You know, I really should notify the police about this," said the fisherman.

"We can appreciate how you feel," said Pete. "I'm in no position to tell you what to do, but you should know that the police were in on trying to drown us. If you report this, you'll put us and possibly yourself in danger. At least give us half a day to straighten this out. All of us but the big Cajun here live right on the island. We're not going anywhere."

"All right. This is all too crazy to be made up. I'll stay out of it."

"Thanks, man, you're doing the right thing."

After being dropped off at Rick's condo, Rick and Walt scurried to the door. As they stood at the door, Rick felt around his nonexistent pockets for keys. Their ride was long gone.

"You got my keys—right, Walt?"

"Yeah, they're with the bottle of scotch I been hidin' in my jockey shorts." They both just smiled at each other. There was no way to break in the condo without calling attention to themselves.

"OK, you want to think up an explanation for how you and I are locked out of my condo with no clothes on?"

"Rick, ain't nobody gonna believe I'm gay. Now you on the other hand…"

"You're not as nice as people say you are," Rick said with a smile.

"I got the answer," Walt said, looking more energetic. "Don't fret another minute, ol' boy. Just follow me. Try not to attract any attention," he said dryly.

Rick and Walter walked past two buildings down to another condominium complex at Palmetto Dunes. Walter led Rick up wooden steps, which were surrounded by a trellis covered by Confederate jasmine in full bloom. The intoxicating aroma filled the staircase. Walter rang the bell after adjusting his blanket.

"Hey, fellas," said Vickie, "Nice outfits."

CHAPTER 35

▼

A priest, who was leading a discussion with a youth group in the picnic area behind the church, kept one eye on Wade and Pete as they exited the fisherman's car. Pete and Wade noticed the priest as well. Pete walked to the far side of his sedan then dropped down to retrieve his key box, mooning Wade in the process.

"Nice ass."

"Thanks for noticing. I've been working out."

Pete tossed the box to Wade so he could open the trunk, which served as a nice shield. They quickly dressed in the clothes they had worn to Walter's. The clothing felt good against Pete's cold skin. Wade placed the safety on his handgun before jamming it into his right front pant pocket.

"The padre over there looks nervous," said Pete, as he peered around the trunk lid.

"Screw it. Just act like you belong here and don't look at him. Let's have that phone."

As Wade dialed up Marcus Fisher, his FBI contact in Charleston, the priest walked with the youth group to the church. Still sleeping after a late night bust in the historic district, Marcus answered in a fog.

"Yo Marcus, it's Wade."

"You back in the Big Easy?"

"No. I'm still on Hilton Head. Listen. That number you got us led to some bad dudes. We were knee-deep in 'gators last night. We're diggin' out now, but I need your help again. The local sheriff is dirty. I need some agents from Charleston or Savannah to get over here before somebody gets killed. What can you do?"

"I can come with some guys in a few hours. I gotta have somethin' more if we're gonna come running."

"How about attempted murder by the local sheriff and embezzlement by local officials and a damn presidential candidate?"

Pete cringed when Wade referred to Buddy.

"I thought you were on vacation?" Marcus said.

"Yeah, I was. I'm gonna need another one after all this shit. Just get down here as soon as you can."

The tall man and the short man traveled north along the shore in their inflatable boat and stopped at Foley Field Beach. As the boat touched the beach, the tall man jumped onto the sand and pushed the boat back to sea in the process. The short man headed back to the shrimp boat. Carrying a small duffel, the tall man ran to the public bathroom to change into a casual shirt, slacks, and lightweight jacket. A man who was searching for lost jewelry with a metal detector, a tall brunette with her golden retriever, and the seagulls paid little attention. As he emerged from the restroom, he tossed his old clothing into the trash, attempted to brush the wrinkles out of his new outfit, and started his 20-minute walk to the hospital.

Pete and Wade entered the woods and followed the rope they laid before. Tired and still cold, Pete was less enthused about this trip through the woods than the last one. He knew, however, that this trip was necessary to save his hide and his career. Gibby and Carver would claim ignorance of the entire incident and brand the four private investigators as lunatics who were trying to find a scapegoat for the accident that killed Clay Stevens. Because of a corrupt sheriff, they would need to commit more crimes in order to clear themselves and bring Morton Bennett, Gibby Morgan, Larry Carver, and possibly Buddy Duke to justice. The two stopped two-thirds of the way into the woods, where they could see that Carver was sitting at his desk and working at the computer. Cutting around through the woods to the far edge of the parking lot, they escaped detection. Because it was Saturday morning, the lot held only Carver's Impala. Moving quickly, they entered the administration area. Wade pulled the revolver from his pocket.

"We back from the dead, Carver," said Wade in a menacing voice.

"What the hell?" yelled Carver, looking as if he had seen a ghost. "How did you two survive?"

"You and Gibby are idiots," said Pete. "Everybody with a boat knows that there are sandbars miles offshore. It took us a while but we found one. The water was only five feet at low tide."

Pete walked to the fake ficus tree in the corner of the office and pulled the computer disk from the mulch. Holding it with two fingers, he waved the disk in front of Carver.

"And what's that supposed to be?" said Carver defiantly.

"This is going to send all you bastards to jail."

"What are you going to do with me?" asked Carver, in a less defiant tone.

"You're gonna swim with the sharks, my man," said Pete, as he winked at Wade.

"OK, Pete. We need to find a place to hide out with this sorry sack of shit until the FBI shows up."

"We'll go to Clay's. They key is under the mat."

Pete and Wade led Carver to the parking lot and into the woods. After walking a third of the way into the woods, they could see a police cruiser parked next to Pete's car. Deputy Lacy stood next to the cruiser, talking on the radio as he ran the plate through the computer to identify the owner. The mud on the plate made the situation even more suspicious.

"Damn," said Pete. "What now?" The lack of sleep, fatigue from hypothermia, and treading water were catching up with him. He was used to staying up all night at work, but this felt like two nights with no sleep between.

"We turn around and take Carver's car."

Carver's attempt to yell for the deputy was thwarted by a quick punch to the groin from Wade. Carver dropped to his knees and turned green.

"Get up, asshole. Do that again and you'll be singin' in the girls' choir. You *are* a dumb shit," said Wade in a harsh whisper.

The three turned back to the parking lot undetected by the deputy. As they crossed the lot, a tall clean-cut young man emerged from the administration building. The man walked directly toward them. Hoping to avoid an encounter, Wade steered them toward Carver's car.

"Excuse me, I'm looking for Mr. Larry Carver," said the tall man as he halted 30 feet away from the group.

"That's me," said Carver, anticipating another hit in the groin.

"I need to speak with you. Can we talk in your office?"

"That won't be possible," said Wade. "We late for an important appointment now."

"It's possible," said the man as he pulled a handgun from a vest holster. I want all three of you to come into Mr. Carver's office with me."

"Who you workin' for?" asked Wade.

"That doesn't concern you. Just do as I say."

"What you want with Carver?" Wade probed.

"We have business to discuss and it's in your best interest to come with me," said the tall man, growing irritated.

Deputy Jack Gurba walked from the hospital morgue, where he had just viewed the bodies of Morton Bennett, Tami Bennett, and Gibby Morgan. Dumbfounded by these apparently unrelated deaths, he awaited the arrival of detectives from Beaufort. Shaken by the loss of his boss, he headed to the administration area. He hoped to find Carver to inform him of the death of the hospital board chairman. While walking toward Carver's office, Gurba spied Pete and the others in the parking lot. At least he had one mystery solved.

"Hey, doc. Where have you been?" said Gurba as he walked out the door.

Thoughts raced through Pete's head. *Is Gurba clean? What does he know? Is he in with the tall man in the suit? What in hell are we doing here?*

As Gurba approached, the tall man turned on his heels and fired a shot into Gurba's chest. Gurba fell as if his feet were pulled from under him. His head struck the concrete with the sound of a bowling ball's hitting the wood deck. The sound of his head as it hit the parking lot was louder than that emitted from the silencer on the gun. As Gurba lay motionless, blood flowed from the back of his head onto the pavement. Wade, Pete, and Carver dropped to the ground. Pete wasn't sure why, but it seemed to be a good idea at the time. Before the tall man in the suit could turn back to the three men, a gunshot stung their ears and hit the tall man in the right thigh. He fell to the ground, wincing in pain, and dropped the gun at his side. He let out a loud cry, and grabbed his blood-soaked leg. Wade ran to the tall man and kicked him in the face before retrieving his weapon. The tall man writhed on the pavement, his thigh burning and his broken nose bleeding. Wade looked for the shooter while he moved to check on Gurba. Pete pushed Carver flat on the ground and twisted his arm to ensure compliance.

"He's got a pulse. Stay with Carver. I'm gonna run in and call 911," said Wade.

"Wade, we're at the damn hospital. I'll just call up to the ER and have them bring down some stretchers. You hold the village idiot while I call on my phone."

"Both of you stay where you are," said Deputy Lacy from the edge of the woods. "Drop your weapons and take five steps toward me."

Wade put down the two guns and kicked them off to the side. Both Wade and Pete stood with hands held out to the side and slowly walked toward Lacy. *Is this one clean?* If he was clean, they were home free. If he was in with Gibby Morgan, they were up to their asses in alligators again. Pete's heart raced as the adrenaline flowed. He was running on fumes, he wasn't sure how much more excitement he could endure.

"Lacy, it's me, Peter Fredericks from the ER."

"I know it's you, doc. Do what I told you. I can't take any chances. I need to figure out what's going on."

"I can appreciate that, man. I'm confused myself. Let me call up to the ER so we can get Gurba and this other guy some medical attention."

"OK, doc. Go ahead and call."

Lacy called for backup while Pete spoke with one of the ER nurses.

"Who did *you* shoot?" said Lacy, pointing at Wade.

"I didn't shoot nobody. This guy shot the deputy," pointing at the tall man. "I thought *you* shot this guy," Wade said, pointing at the tall man.

"That's right," Pete added.

"I haven't fired my weapon," said the deputy.

"Well, who in hell shot him?" said Wade.

"I did," said a voice from behind a car 50 feet away.

"Who's that?" said Lacy. "Come out where I can see you and put down your weapon."

"It's Victoria Jackson. Don't shoot."

Victoria emerged from behind the car with her hands in the air. She wore camouflage pants and tall lace-up boots. Wearing a tight-fitting black shirt and her hair in a ponytail, she looked as if she stepped out of some upscale hunting catalog.

"Vickie, what are you doing involved in this mess?" Lacy said. "Come stand with the doc and this other guy."

"Lacy, let me help Gurba," pleaded Pete. "Wade Boudreaux here is ex-FBI. He can explain everything. Mr. Carver here and Gibby Morgan tried to drown us last night after we uncovered their dirty deeds. I have no idea who this other guy is. I think he wanted to kill Carver."

"All right. Go help Gurba. Is he alive?"

"He had a pulse a couple of minutes ago."

As Pete knelt over Gurba, two nurses with stretchers and another deputy wheeled around the corner.

"Dr. Fredericks! What's going on here?" cried one of the nurses.

"It's too complicated to explain now. Let's get Gurba on a stretcher and up to the ER. He's been shot in the chest."

"I'm OK, doc," said Gurba groggily. I had my vest on."

"You sure have a habit of cracking your head open right in front of me. Come on, we still have to fix your head and get a CAT scan like we did before. You were out cold for three minutes."

Pete grabbed a bed sheet from the stretcher, tore it, and wrapped it around Gurba's head to control the bleeding. They lifted him to the stretcher to be wheeled up to the ER.

"Get a CAT scan, chest x-ray, and set up a tray to suture his head. I'll be up in a few minutes."

"What about me?" cried the tall man.

"We're not going to let you bleed to death. You're one of our star witnesses. You're going to help send Mr. Carver here to jail along with the Bennetts and Sheriff Morgan."

"One out of four ain't bad," said Lacy.

"What do you mean?" said Pete, looking more confused.

"The Bennetts were shot dead this morning and Gibby killed himself," said Lacy.

"Can you believe that shit?" said Wade.

"Don't be so sure about Gibby killing himself," said Pete. "If this dude wanted Carver dead then he wanted the others dead, too."

"So who wants 'em dead?" Wade asked.

"Buddy Duke, I guess," Pete shrugged. He finally admitted to himself that Buddy had sold him out. He hung his head.

They loaded the tall man in the suit onto the stretcher, and the deputy handcuffed him to the rail after frisking him.

"You three have a lot of explaining to do," said Lacy. "You come inside with me so I can start taking statements. The detectives will be here from Beaufort in a little while."

"FBI is coming, too," said Wade.

"Excuse me?" said Lacy.

"We called them 'cause we didn't know who we could trust in your office with that sheriff bein' dirty and all."

"Whatever you say," said an exasperated Lacy, throwing his arms in the air and motioning for them to walk inside.

"That was some nice shootin', Vickie dawlin'. What were you aimin' for?"

"I was aiming for what I hit, Wade Boudreaux. If I was fixin' to kill him, I would have hit him 'tween the eyes."

"Victoria, I didn't know you could shoot," said Pete.

"I told you there were lots of things you didn't know about me. My daddy was a better hunter than a fisherman. He taught me well. I can shoot a beer bottle off a fencepost at a hundred yards in a high wind."

"Damn, Cheré. You got any other hidden talents?" asked Wade.

"None you'll ever see," she said with a wink.

"How'd you know to come to the hospital?" said Pete.

"When I saw Rick and Walter, I put two and two together. After you almost got yourselves killed last night, I figured you might need some help. Oh, shit. I almost forgot. Pete, I gotta tell you somethin' else. We can't find Molly. Debbie said she went out to look for you this morning."

Pete's heart sank. The thought of losing Molly because of his foolish plans could not be fathomed. The rage welled. He ran up to Carver and Lacy as they approached the doors to the administration building. He slammed Carver into the glass, and Carver fell in a slump.

"Doc, what are you doing?" yelled Lacy.

"Where is my wife?" Pete seethed. He traded glances with Wade. Carver said nothing. Wade pulled his fist back.

"On three, your head and that door become one," Wade said calmly.

"OK. She's on Betts' yacht. They're probably leaving for Bermuda now."

Pete thrust his knee into Carver's face. "That's for killing my dog, asshole." Carver fell over as blood flowed from his deformed nose.

There was no time for them to learn about Betts' OxyContin operation or who was involved in it. Pete looked at Vickie and Wade.

"If we go in there, we lose Molly."

CHAPTER 36

▼

Pete, Wade, and Vickie tore across the lot and into the woods. By the time Lacy could handcuff Carver, the three had run half way to Pete's car.

"Hey. Stop," Lacy yelled. "You three get back here. Aw, come on. Gimme a break."

Lacy could not leave a crime scene with a man in handcuffs and a wounded prisoner. He called for backup from Beaufort and lifted Carver to his feet. The three fugitives piled into Pete's car and headed to the marina.

"What now?" Vickie asked, breathless from the run.

"There's only one course to Bermuda," Wade said. "We gonna set that course and hope we catch 'em."

Pete slammed his fist against the dash. "Son of a bitch. I can't believe this shit. I'm gonna kill Betts. He's gonna hang from a damn tree like they did my dog."

"Take it easy, now," Wade said. "We need to stay focused here."

"I'm not taking it goddamn easy, Wade. I'm about to lose the only thing in my life that has any meaning right now."

"You right. I'm sorry. We too tired for all this shit. But we gonna do what it takes to get Molly back."

"Whose boat are we going to use?" Vickie urged.

"I think Gibby won't be usin' his today," Wade said.

Not knowing if they were being pursued, Wade created a parking space on the far side of the marina building and they scooted unnoticed down to Gibby's boat. As he stepped into the boat, Pete noticed that Gibby had cleaned his boat of any remnants of the attempted murders but failed to refuel. A half tank remained and he had no idea how far that would get them.

"You know how to hot-wire a boat?" Pete said, as Vickie and Wade stepped down into the boat.

"Boats are easy. Find me a tool box while I find the right wires."

Wade could barely fit his wide torso into the opening of the console to find the wires. After several rounds of wire cutting and stripping, Wade connected the wires, which brought the twin engines to life.

"I don't know why they even have keys for these things. A monkey could do that," Wade said, shaking his head as he lifted his large frame off the deck.

"Anybody know how to work these navigation gizmos?" Pete asked anxiously.

"I'll take a crack at it," Vickie said, taking the instruction manual from Pete.

"See if you can figure out his navigation system and set us a course for Bermuda," Pete said, as he untied the craft from the thick pilings.

At full speed, Pete followed the green markers of the Intracoastal Waterway to the north end of the island and turned east into Port Royal Sound—the sound that was big enough to hold the royal navy. Hidden by dense pine forest were Parris Island on the left and Hilton Head Plantation and Port Royal Plantation on the right. The swells grew larger as they approached the open ocean. The adrenaline kept Pete from having what would normally cause intense seasickness. They headed due east until Vickie figured out the navigation system.

"There you go," Vickie said with pride. "Keep the little boat between the two lines on the screen and we'll stay on course for Bermuda."

More like the middle of the ocean, Pete thought, as he adjusted his course. The gas would not last forever. Now that he had time to think, anger at Carver, the Bennetts, Duke, and now Betts swelled inside. Duke pissed him off the most.

While they were still in range for the cell phone, Wade rang up Marcus Fisher. "Yo, Marcus. Got a spare helicopter?"

"What are you up to now?" Marcus asked suspiciously.

"We in a fishin' boat tryin' to outrun a yacht with a hostage on it. They headed for Bermuda. Not sure how far out they are."

"Look, man. I sent four agents down to Hilton Head. I tie up another agent, a pilot, and a chopper, and this thing don't pan out, my ass is grass."

"Marcus, you gotta trust me on this. It's my buddy's wife bein' held on that yacht. We might run out of gas before we catch 'em. Come on. Kidnappin' is a federal crime, ain't it?"

"I'll be in the air in 20 minutes. Gimme your GPS coordinates, your speed, and your heading."

The operator of the OxyContin lab also served as the captain of Betts' yacht. He set the controls to autopilot and went below to check on Betts.

"Dr. Betts, I have to slow down now if we are going to have enough fuel to make it."

"Do what you must," Betts said dejectedly as he sat at the dining table and rubbed his temples. He hoped that Coswell's plan to eliminate the others would allow him to return when things calmed down. He didn't like having a hostage and he never expected to be making a last-minute dash away from the island.

"Where is the girl?"

"I lock her in room at front of boat," Betts said. "I took gag off but arms and legs are still tied."

"I'll be up top if you need me," the captain said.

Wade could see the captain as he backed his way out of the cabin but they weren't close enough yet for a good shot. As the captain turned, Wade could tell he had spotted them. Wade braced his arm on the windshield and fired. The bullet splintered the fiberglass of the cabin. The captain scrambled on his hands and knees to take cover in front of the cabin.

"You two stay low. We gonna get shot at."

The captain lay on his belly and yelled down to the cabin through the vent to Betts. Quickly a handgun appeared through the opening. The captain squirmed to the side of the cabin and rose to one knee. He fired one shot, which glanced off the frame of the windshield. Sparks flew and the Plexiglas splintered. Wade didn't flinch. Before the captain could fire again, Wade leaned around the side of the boat, brought his sites over the chest of the captain, and killed him with a single shot to the heart.

"Nice shot," Vickie said as she patted Wade on the shoulder.

"It looks like that yacht is on autopilot," Wade said. We're gonna have to get up next to it and jump on."

"Don't make it sound so easy," Pete yelled over the sound of the engines.

"Come on, man. If we miss, you'll swing back around and get me."

"I can do it," Vickie said with conviction.

"Oh, no. I'm not letting you take that risk," Pete said, putting his palm in the air.

"Come on. You two are fried. You've been up for over a day and spent half the night treading water. I'm fresh and I know I can do it. Plus, Wade, I've seen you hobble around on your knees."

"This is a bad idea," Pete said, shaking his head back and forth.

Wade stepped right up into Pete's face and firmly grasped his shoulder. "Look, friend. You want your wife back, we gotta do this." He tapped the gas gauge with his finger. Pete nodded.

Vickie zipped Wade's pistol into her jacket pocket. Wade tightened her life vest and helped steady her on the bow railing. Pete pounded through the wake of the yacht and inched toward the port side. Each time they hit a swell, the fishing boat lurched. Wade steadied Vickie's legs as she tried to time her move with the ocean swells. She reached up over her head to the metal side railing of the yacht and grabbed tightly with both hands. A large swell pushed the boat into the yacht with a dull thud. A gigantic spray erupted as the water was forced between the two crafts. Pete overcorrected and steered too far away from the yacht. Vickie's legs flipped into the air and then slammed against the side of the yacht. Vickie dangled off the side of the yacht like a mooring buoy. Wade motioned for Pete to get back under her. Vickie pumped her legs trying to get footing on the smooth fiberglass. As they neared, Wade held out his big paws to steady Vickie, but she lost her grip and fell into the white foam.

By the time she popped back up, breathless and screaming in pain, the two boats were 50 yards away. Pete looked at the gas gauge and he looked at Vickie in the mirror. If he turned around, there would be no gas for another try. Somebody was probably going to die no matter what he did. Wade looked at him and held his arms out from his sides. Pete thought about Molly and he thought about the pain he experienced when he had hit the cold water before. All he could do was go back to what he knew from medicine—treat the sickest patient first. He pulled back on the throttle and turned the boat around. It took a full minute to get back to Vickie, who was swinging her arms back and forth in the air when they arrived. Pete put the engines in hard reverse as they coasted up to Vickie, which nearly caused Wade to tumble over the railing. The two leaned over the edge of the boat and hauled Vickie out of the water.

"Shit. I thought you weren't coming back for a minute there. Damn, I'm sorry I lost my grip."

"Don't worry about it," Pete said. "We gave it our best shot."

"You say that like we're done," Vickie said, shivering. "Come on, we'll try again."

"Yeah, let's go," Wade said.

"No, it's too dangerous," Pete's voice was cracking.

"You let us be the judge of that," Wade said, stepping past Pete. "It's no damn use fussin' about it while we sit here." Wade sat down in the driver's seat and pushed the throttles forward. The engines died.

CHAPTER 37

▼

Pete leaned his head against the railing and broke down. To be so close and then lose Molly was worse than not getting to the yacht at all. He kicked himself for not taking time to get more fuel before leaving. He kicked himself for getting into the whole mess in the first place. Wade and Victoria rallied around him and tried to encourage him. Pete could tell that Vickie was freezing.

"Vickie, I'm sorry. Here I am having my little pity party and you're about to freeze to death. We have to get you out of these clothes." Vickie looked at him out of the corner of her eyes. Pete cracked a smile. "Come on, you know what I mean. Go in the cabin and see what you can find."

Vickie shivered her way down into the cabin while Pete and Wade huddled by the transom.

"Listen, we not outta this game yet," Wade said, putting his arm around Pete's shoulder. "My buddy Marcus is gonna come through."

"How are they going to get on that yacht from a helicopter?" Pete asked, unconvinced.

Wade had no clue. He didn't want Pete to be discouraged, though. "Oh, they got ways. It depends on what kinda chopper they got. Listen, I screwed up. I'm sorry."

"We both screwed up pretty bad. Let's see if we can fix it. You game?"

"I'm always game," Wade said as he hugged Pete with one arm.

Vickie emerged from the cabin wearing yellow rain pants and an old paint-stained sweatshirt. Both were three sizes too big, requiring her to roll up the sleeves and legs.

"Man, you are one sexy broad. You wear that outfit down on the bayou, they'd jump ya bones right on the pier."

"From you, Wade, I'll take that as a compliment. So what's the plan?"

"We sit and wait until the cavalry comes," Wade said, dropping down onto the deck to lean against the transom.

Pete and Vickie did the same and all three sat in a row with their legs stretched out. Pete thought of the ride out to sea with Gibby and Carver. It still amazed him they survived it. A thunderclap brought him back to reality. They could see the edge of the storm as it moved towards them. Lightning flashed in the distance and the sea began to roll more. Pete knew that the storm was going to complicate things if the helicopter didn't come soon. They sat in silence for several minutes.

"So, Wade, besides being nearly drowned last night, how do you like Hilton Head?" Vickie asked.

"Aside from that, this place is pretty nice. I think I had enough of Naw'lins. Maybe I'll just move here."

"Would your wife like that?"

"Here's the deal with my wife, Vickie. She be dead from cancer soon. It's all over her body like stink on a damn dead fish. I'm not the brightest dude, but I know she's about at the end. We came here to see this cancer doctor for a final try. Now we know that's a bunch a shit. When she's gone, I probably leave Louisiana and make a new life."

"I'll vote for you if you run for sheriff," Pete said.

"Yeah, me too," Vickie added.

"A Cajun sheriff on Hilton Head—now that's somethin' that'll scare away the tourists," Wade said.

Pete stood and turned toward the mainland. "Listen."

"I don't hear nothin'."

"Me either."

"Be still now. That's the sound of helicopter rotors," Pete said, suddenly full of energy.

"OK, I can hear it now," Vickie said as she stood up.

"Man, you must be part dog," Wade said, peering into the distance.

"No, you probably have five years of wax in those ears."

"That's about the last time I saw a doctor."

Pete, Wade, and Vickie watched the FBI helicopter zip by in the distance.

"Well, shit. Are they not looking for us?" Vickie said.

CHAPTER 38

▼

As the Coast Guard HH-65 Dolphin recovery helicopter cleared the Savannah coast, Lieutenant Wally Glosser adjusted his course for the coordinates given to him by Marcus Fisher.

"Rev. You ready for rescue checklist part one?" Wally said over the internal communication system.

Rev was short for Reverend, Petty Officer Billy Souder's nickname. Nobody was quite sure how he got it, but he was stuck with it. Wally was in charge but, as the flight mechanic, Rev called most of the shots. He finished swinging out the hoist and he opened the hatch above the side door.

"Yes, sir. Ready for part one."

While Rev followed the checklist with the pilots, Petty Officer Chip Swonger made some final adjustments on his Tri-SAR harness and performed his radio check when prompted by Rev. As the rescue swimmer, the harness allowed him to attach to the braided stainless-steel cable in the hoist so he could be lowered to the water. Tethered by his gunner's belt, he kneeled near the open door and scanned the ocean with his binoculars for their target.

"Three o'clock, Wally," Chip said as he found the disabled fishing boat.

"Good eyes, Chipper. I'll see if I can raise them on their radio." Wally switched to channel 16. "Rescue 6553 to disabled craft. Do you read?"

"I read you, Rescue 6553. This is Wade Boudreaux. Go ahead."

"Is anyone injured?"

"No, don't worry about us. Jus' follow that yacht and get the hostage."

"The FBI is in pursuit of the yacht. We need to lift the three of you off right now before the storm hits. We can't do much from the air until the FBI stops the yacht. Stand by."

While Wally approached the fishing boat, Rev completed rescue checklist part two. He connected Chip to the hook.

"Rescue check part two complete. Ready aft for direct deployment," Rev said calmly.

"Go on hot mic. Check swimmer," Wally directed, as he lowered to 25 feet above the waterline.

As the helicopter approached the boat, the sound increased from a low-pitched beating to a deafening high-pitched whine from the tail rotor. The 40-foot rotors whipped the air and water around them as the three watched the pilot position the bright orange craft. Wally turned into the wind and held his position.

"On hot mic. Checking swimmer," Rev said, as he tugged on Chip's harness, and Chip disconnected from his gunner's belt. "Swimmer ready."

"Conn me in," Wally said.

Now came the crucial teamwork between the flight mechanic and the pilot. The pilot could not see the boat. The flight mechanic could see, but he could not do his job and fly the helicopter simultaneously.

"Come 20 feet AWL and 30 feet right."

Wally smoothly lowered the helicopter five feet and eased toward the boat. Rev held Chip's harness with a death grip until it was time to deploy.

"Easy right," Rev said, as he picked up the hoist pendant. "Hold position."

Rev lowered Chip to the boat. Without a hello, Chip stepped up to Vickie and yelled, "You're first." All Vickie could do was nod. Chip slipped the rescue strop around Vickie and positioned it properly. He gave the thumbs up to Rev and pulled Vickie in close. They made eye contact the whole way up. With a big grin on his face, Rev helped Vickie out of the harness and directed her to the cave-like area in the back of the helicopter. Pete was next and then Wade. They left the boat to drift. By the time all three settled in, the pilot had entered coordinates for the yacht that he got from Marcus Fisher.

Pete fidgeted while Chip passed out ear plugs. Chip kneeled next to Vickie and leaned in so his nose almost touched her ear.

"I hope I didn't scare you, ma'am," Chip yelled in his twangy Texas accent. He placed his hand over hers. "We don't like to spend any more time out on that hook than we have to."

"Oh, I understand. I feel…I felt very safe. And it's Vickie. You don't have to call me ma'am."

"Man, he is a stud, isn't he Rev? Let's save the small talk for the All Ranks Club at the base," Wally said. "Chip, get some more info from them about this yacht."

Pete and Wade took turns telling Chip about Betts and his hostage. As they approached the yacht at 95 knots, rain started to whip through the side door.

The pilot radioed to Marcus Fisher. "Rescue 6553, FBI One."

"FBI One. Go ahead."

"I've got the target on radar."

"That's good, Rescue, 'cause we're buggin out," Marcus said. "This storm is about to pitch us in the drink. Oh, shit. Looks like the hostage just went off the back end."

"Stay with your survivor. Let the yacht go. Be there in two minutes."

Pete could tell there was a problem by the looks on the faces of the crew. He hung his head and squeezed his friends' hands.

"I've got visual on you, FBI One. As soon as we get visual on the hostage, you clear out."

"Roger that."

"Three miles east and you'll be back out of it," Wally said without emotion. "You have clearance to land as CGAS Savannah—Approach Control is 118.4. We'll catch up to you when we recover the hostage. Fly safe now."

"She's not moving," Swonger barked. "I'm doin' a physical grip."

They quickly positioned over Molly and performed the checklist. Chip gave the thumbs up and in less than a minute, he was in the frigid ocean. A 10-foot wave crested on him and he swung around like a kid on a tire swing. Once he gained sight of Molly again, he swam to her. He put his arms around her chest and looked up at Rev. Waves pounded them as Rev hoisted them up. Blood streamed across Molly's lifeless face.

"She must have hit her head on the way off the yacht," Chip said. "Thank God for the life vest."

They pulled Molly's limp body to the center of the deck and Pete held her close. The guilt and the grief were like a thick hand around his throat that was closing tighter with every breath.

"We'll be leaving that yacht for another day," Wally said, as he turned back to Savannah, and Betts disappeared beyond the horizon.

CHAPTER 39

▼

Pete and Wade drank rum at the poolside bar at the Marriott Hotel on St. Thomas. Elbow to elbow at the bar, their shared hardship bound them together. The gigantic and beautiful Carnival Legend slipped behind them into St. Thomas Harbor to moor for the night. The hotel manager rallied everyone's attention by waving a bottle of rum in the air and announcing a trivia contest. "I've got a bottle of St. Thomas' finest rum for the first one of you drunks to tell me the state bird of Louisiana."

Pete and Wade smiled at each other. "You gonna tell him?"

"It'd be like shootin' fish in a barrel," Wade said.

"It's the Great Egret," yelled some know-it-all from New York City.

"Brrrrp. Wrong. Thanks for playing. Anybody else?

"No, it's the Great Blue Heron," slurred a divorcée from Ohio whose string bikini barely held it all in.

"Nice try, sweetheart. Who's next?"

"Guess I'll have to end the misery." Wade motioned for the manager to come closer. "Brown Pelican."

"That's it—the pelican. We have a winner. What's your name and where ya from?"

Wade filled several shot glasses and passed the bottle around to the crowd.

"There she is," Pete said, elbowing Wade. "Doesn't she look stunning?"

"She is hot," Wade said. "You gonna take advantage of her tonight?"

"You bet."

Pete slid over to make a space and she wiggled in between them.

"Sorry I'm late, boys."

"That's OK, Mol," Wade said. "Have a shot of free St. Thomas rum."

Pete pecked her on the cheek. He thought she looked much sexier after she gained back the 10 pounds she lost. The neurosurgeon had pronounced Molly fully recovered and released her to travel six months after her near-fatal brain injury. The threesome drank until the lights of Charlotte Amalie became a blur. Pete and Molly poured Wade into his bed in 204, and then stumbled to their room next door. Knowing that nobody in Charlotte Amalie could see them through the picture window, Molly stripped while Pete went to the bathroom to relieve himself of what seemed like a gallon of rum. She sat naked on the balcony until Pete figured out where she went. As soon as Pete stretched out on the lounger, Molly straddled him and the attack commenced. She wrestled his clothes off and they reveled in the joy of being alive together.

Wade and Pete awakened by noon. It wasn't noon yet on the east coast, so who cared? Molly begged off going into town. Her plan was to bake on the beach for a few hours and then get a massage. Sex before dinner was implied when she flashed Pete as he left the room.

They got bagels and OJ for the 10-minute trip in the water taxi across St. Thomas Harbor to Charlotte Amalie. The two enjoyed the warmth of the high sun from a cloudless sky as they relaxed on the stern of the boat. The leather-skinned driver droned on about Virgin Island facts. Pete planned to scan the jewelry shops for a tennis bracelet for Molly. Wade planned to eat a huge lunch after that and drink beer.

"Catch any bad guys lately, detective?"

"That's Mr. Detective to you, doc. We nailed some SOB tried to put a hit on his wife. Lives in one of those mansions off island. Had 2 million in term and 1 mil in universal on her. Hit guy gave up the husband when we busted him on some minor traffic thing. Had two unregistered handguns in the car. Big parole violation, so he gave up the husband for leniency. Hilton Head's more interesting than I figured."

"Yeah, didn't take me long to figure out that moving to an island never cured anybody's personality disorder."

"So, ya think Molly's cured now? Still hard to believe she survived it. What you call it again?"

"Epidural hematoma. Yeah, she's done great since the brain surgery to remove the clot. Star patient," Pete said, as they stepped off the taxi onto Veterans Drive.

They strolled among the cruise-ship tourists past the assortment of jewelry shops, clothing stores, bars, and souvenir shops. Fancy yachts of all sizes rested in their slips along the edge of the harbor. The sterns of most faced them. They read the names as they walked. *I Sue 4U*—how original, Pete thought. Probably some asshole personal injury lawyer. *Midnight Dream, Virgin Hopper, Fish Finder,* and the granddaddy of them all, *Walk in the Park.* A thin blonde in a terrycloth robe sat on the transom with what looked like a glass of champagne. The neurosurgeon had told Pete about a reputable jewelry shop on Main. They headed there.

"Molly looks good with short hair—makes her look younger," Wade said.

"I like it, too. Beats being bald. You notice she's a little spunkier than before the accident?"

"She was a damn firecracker last night."

"Tell me about it," Pete said, thinking about the fun and games on the balcony. "I guess we all got the life's too short lesson, huh?"

"Damn straight."

"She's been gone five months now, huh?" Pete said, searching for the right shop. "You never get over it."

"Ya just learn to live with it," they said in unison smiling at each other. Pete patted Wade on the shoulder.

"Walt got me through those first few weeks. Hard to believe, he's even got me goin' to church with him."

"The earth shake when you walked in?"

"Somethin' like that. We shoulda brought ol' Walt. At least I'd have somebody to drink and play cards with while you guys screw on the balcony."

"Heard that, huh? Shit, don't tell Molly."

Pete pointed Wade into a modest store. Simple display cases outlined the room. An olive-skinned man with a thick black mustache smiled broadly at them. Pete dropped the name of the neurosurgeon to the shop owner. Pete figured there must have been some serious exchange of money in the past. The owner acted like they were the Prince and Duke of Hilton Head. They walked out with a four-carat tennis bracelet for about a third of what he would pay in the States. Wade's stomach could be put off no longer, so they found a restaurant near the harbor and sat at the bar.

"So when you gonna give it to her?"

"Birthday is next month. You gonna buy Clay's condo?"

"Gonna wait 'til the old place sells. Then I do it."

A trim young man who had been making time with the comely young bartender leaned over toward Pete and Wade.

"Excuse me. Ya'll from N'awlins?"

"He used to be," Pete pointed his thumb at Wade.

A wide smile came across Luke Guidry's well-tanned face. He dried his hand across his flat belly and shook their hands. "Been gone from Lafayette for about a year now. Good to hear a voice sounds like home."

Luke and Wade slipped into a Cajun dialect that Pete could barely understand. Pete ordered three Red Stripes and some appetizers while the two swapped stories about growing up in Cajun country.

"You two gonna talk English or should I get an interpreter?" Pete handed the beer to Luke. "What's that on your shirt?"

"Logo for the *Walk in the Park*. I'm a mate."

"Yeah, we saw it. She's beautiful."

"You want, I'll take you on a tour. We stuck here least a week 'til our new first mate arrives."

"Like that, Pete? Says he stuck here. How 'bout we get stuck here for an extra week?"

"I meant we supposed to be in St. Kitts now gettin' my boss's new house ready. Got a slip right out the back door."

"What's your boss do?" asked Pete.

"Spend money like it's water. Dude bought a bunch a Dell, Microsoft, and Intel stock before they ran up like crazy. Took a half mil inheritance, turned it into a hundred mil."

"So, what's the hold-up?" Wade said as he motioned for another set of beers.

"First mate died of an overdose of OC. Shit they makin' here is better than you get from the pharmacy."

Pete and Wade looked at each other and smiled knowingly. It was time to move to a booth in the corner and get to know their new friend.

"How you know they makin' OxyContin here?"

"First mate told me his dealer told him. You lookin' to score some?

Pete and Wade spent the next hour taking turns telling parts of their story. Between chapters, they ate fried frog legs, calamari, Portobello mushrooms, goat-cheese tarts, shrimp and scallops over angel hair pasta, and grilled swordfish.

"So, we lost Betts. We figured cops in Bermuda would get him. He never showed," Wade said before stuffing in the last bite of bread pudding in rum sauce. "Wanna help us find this tick on the butt a humanity?"

"Why not? We just killin' time this week. We not 'sposed to be havin' parties but the captain does it anyway. Come as my guest tonight. That dealer might be there."

"You sure? Don't wanna mess up plans with missy at the bar over there," Wade said as he handed the check to Pete.

"We got the whole night."

CHAPTER 40

▼

Pete handed the binoculars to Molly as he and Wade pulled chairs to either side of her. "See that big yacht right next to the tall flagpole?" She sat up and adjusted the focus while scanning the waterfront.

"Yeah, there's some chesty blonde who is sunbathing topless across the bow."

"Lemme see." Wade grabbed the binoculars and quickly realized that Molly had zinged him. "That's a good one, cheré."

"So, what about it?"

Pete hesitated and met eyes with Wade. "We met one of the mates at lunch in town. He's a Cajun boy. He and Wade struck up a conversation. He wants us to come meet his girlfriend tonight."

"Liar. You two are up to something. I can tell."

Wade threw an ice cube at Pete. "Knew I shoulda told her. You can't lie to save ya mama's ass." Wade filled Molly in on the details. She listened intently, no facial expressions. Pete figured she'd be pissed and cut him off for the rest of the week.

"All right. Let's do it. Maybe if I'm in this from the start, you two won't get dropped in the ocean again." Wade wagged his finger at Pete and moved his mouth while Molly talked. Molly could see Wade's mocking her out of the corner of her eye. "Don't you sass me, Wade Boudreaux." Before Wade could react, Molly flipped his chair back into the pool. She sat back down and smiled at Pete. "So, what did you buy in town?"

"Just browsing."

"Liar."

"I know you part coon dog," Wade said in mock indignation as he splashed Molly.

The three huddled in the bow of the water taxi and reviewed their scheme for the evening. The red fireball settled below the hills behind Charlotte Amalie. Long shadows fell from tall masts in the harbor. The heavy beat from some dance tune skipped across the placid water from the *Walk in the Park.*

"Listen now, missy. I know you been feelin' pretty good lately. Don't get smart with this guy. These dealers don't give a shit 'bout nobody. Plenty a deep ocean to dump all of us."

"I'll be good, Detective."

"Stay in sight. Don't let him get you alone. Be cool. He resists, make like you don't give two shits."

They stepped on to the lower deck of the 200-foot floating mansion. The dozen revelers they could see paid no mind, so they stepped up to the main deck. No sign of Luke. To Pete, the yacht looked like it was launched the week before. Everything clean and polished. No musty smell like most boats.

"Put your tongue back in your mouth. You look like you're gonna drool." Molly jabbed Wade in the side.

"Damn, those girls look like they just walked outa some underwear catalog— Victoria's Mystery."

"Victoria's Secret. And it's lingerie."

"Yeah, Mol, whatever. Man, that chick in the white sundress is hot."

"Get your horse back in the stable there, stud," Pete wagged his index toward Wade's belt. "That dude talking to Miss America has a mate's shirt. Wanna ask him about Luke?"

As Wade slipped over to the starboard side, Luke busted out of the living room with his bartender friend in tow. Both had taken full advantage of the free booze and what smelled like some reefer, too.

Top of his lungs, "Wade, where y'at, man?" Luke motioned for Pete and Molly. They got drinks and made party talk for a while. The Cajun boys sprinkled the conversation with stories of the bayou. Luke's girl of the week excused herself to the head and promised to return with drinks. Luke became sober like flipping a switch. It amazed Pete.

"OK, Molly. Your mark's in the living room. Short little shit. Silk t-shirt, black slacks, shaved head. People been scorin' OC's all evening. I told him you were cool. He thinks you lookin' for five or 10. Forties go for 30 bucks each, eighties for 50. Cash. No refunds."

Pete slipped Molly 200 dollars in 10s. It surprised him how cool she was. Molly found the head near the bow and did her business. She wet her hair some and mussed it a little to look more the part. She came through the living room on the opposite side from Pete and Wade and sat next to the dealer, extending her hand. "Hi, I'm Molly," playfully.

"Good evening, Miss Molly," in a lilting Caribbean accent. "Derek at your service. What are you into today?"

"Oh, I'm just soaking up rays and letting life wash over me this week."

"You're a beautiful lady. Love that hair."

"Yeah, it's my new thing. I had a little accident and they had to shave my head for brain surgery."

"My, I bet that hurt."

"I still get some monster headaches. Luke tells me you're the man to see about that." She turned towards him and crossed her legs Indian style.

"You into the forties or the eighties?"

"I'll have as many forties as this 200 will get me."

"For seven it would be 210 American. Since you are so beautiful, I will give them to you for 200."

"Why thank you, Derek. You're so much nicer than those east-coast dealers. We may have to do some mail-order business."

Wade caught Pete by the arm. "She's fine. Don't get into his line a sight. I can see the back a her head from here."

"This is freakin' me out. I don't like her being so close to this guy."

"Relax," putting his arm around Pete's shoulder. "This is child's play. Molly's a big girl. She'll know when to walk away."

"Yes, we should do that," Derek handing her a business card. "We put them inside cheap souvenirs."

"Why not just send it straight from the east coast?"

"The product is not on the east coast."

"Riiight," Molly said, shaking her head and smiling.

Derek leaned forward and put his hand on her knee. "We could use some more representation back in the States. You'd be good at it."

"Now there's an idea." Molly waved the business card with her hand. "I'll get back to you on that. Thanks, Derek," patting him on the shoulder as she walked out. She stepped down to the lower deck and exited to the street. The boys let her get half way to the water taxi before they took three beers for the road. Wade winked at Luke on the way out.

Molly filled them in as they waited for the taxi. "That was perfect, girl. You a natural at this undercover stuff. Now we gotta get this dude to tell you where they make the shit."

Pete held up his hand. "I hate to spoil the party here, but I don't think any of us should be getting closer to our man, Derek." Pete stood and faced them. "Wade, what's the likelihood he's going to just give up that location to Molly?"

"Not too high. She'd have to get pretty close. You right, we gettin' a little carried away here. Lemme think about this over some beers at the pool."

CHAPTER 41

▼

The next day, Wade crossed the harbor to Charlotte Amalie to visit the government building. Too early in the day for most tourists, he passed only a few businessmen and kids in uniform on their way to school. Still trying to clear the cobwebs from the previous night of drinking, he stopped in a small café for a cup of coffee. The well-tanned business owner flipped through the newspaper, seeming to enjoy some quiet before his busy time started.

"So, how long you been in business here?"

"Coming up on 10 years since I quit my job at the bank in Jersey. Sailed over here with 20 grand in my pocket."

"It take you long to start makin' enough to live?" Wade leaned over the counter and acted more interested.

"'Bout six months. I was lucky, though. I got this place for a song. Established business, owner got sick. I spruced things up, started serving coffee that didn't taste like battery acid. Now I'm happy."

Wade introduced himself and explained his purpose. In his line of work, he learned to be a master at deception. Passing himself off as someone who was looking to start a business, he gathered information about licenses, taxes, and other mundane business issues. Most importantly, he got the name of the clerk he needed to talk to at the government building.

"She's a beautiful Brit. I'll ring Margaret and tell her you're coming."

Taking his coffee and a sweet roll to go, Wade took his time walking to the government building. He fit in well. No camera or dumb T-shirt or zinc oxide on his nose. Island casual. He stuck his head into a small office on the third floor.

"You Margaret?"

"Yes, you must be Wade," in a British accent. She sat among stacks of papers and official-looking books. Only a picture of a cat on her desk.

"I hear you the one to talk to about startin' a business."

"Come in. I'll be happy to help you."

He held a gaze with her green eyes long enough to bring out a broad smile. Dentistry in England was living up to its bad reputation. "I don't want to take up too much of your time. I'd like to talk to people that started businesses, say, in the last six months. Then I come back and see you if I'm still interested."

They talked for 20 minutes and she gave him brochures and more information than he wanted. She packed it all together in a folder for him.

"Come back even if you're not interested," she said with a wink.

She had printed a spreadsheet of business names and locations. Wade studied it as he walked with extra bounce in his step back to the waterfront. He sat on a bench near the *Walk in the Park* and rang Pete with his cell phone.

"Did I interrupt anything good?"

"Just missed. Where are you?"

"In town, playin' detective. Had a brainstorm."

"Don't hurt yourself. Sun up yet?"

"Yeah, 'bout three hours now. Get outa bed. We got work to do. Listen, I'm gonna give you some names a businesses. Stop me if somethin' sounds right."

"Go."

"Templeton Properties Inc., Offshore Limited, Gold Imaginations, Calibogue Enterprises."

Pete's skin tingled and he sat up in bed. For the first time since the day they lost Betts, he felt fear. He walked to the balcony and wondered if he really wanted to find him again. Molly recovered completely and so had their relationship. The last thing he wanted to do was jeopardize it all. "Calibogue is the sound at the south end of Hilton Head."

"Get dressed. I'll meet ya'll at the water taxi drop off."

Pete and Wade stood at the waterfront, trying to find Brewers Bay Road on the map. Now they looked like tourists. They found it north of the airport. Too far to walk.

"Hey, there's no loitering here," an official-sounding voice came from behind. They both jumped like two teenagers looking at *Playboy*.

"Damn, Luke, you gonna give me a heart attack. Let's throw him in, Pete."

"Now, you don't want to do anythin' rash, boys." Luke stepped up between them. "I overheard a little conversation Derek was havin' on his cell phone. Seems they moving some product outa this harbor tonight."

"Let's take a cab ride," Wade said, putting his arm around Luke and heading him back to the road.

Wade filled in Luke during the five-minute ride. "So, how tough is it to bribe a cop here?"

"'Bout as tough as finding a hooker on Bourbon Street," Luke smiled, remembering a raucous weekend in New Orleans. "They're not all dirty, so you'd have to be careful. What you need from the cops?"

The cabby dropped the three at a row of small warehouses. "Nothin'. What I'm thinkin' is that Betts has the locals in his pocket just like in Hilton Head. We been down that damn street once already."

"Yeah, we learned our lesson the hard way," Pete chimed in.

"We can't risk gettin' sideways with the cops. What you say we interrupt their little shipment tonight and see what information we can get?"

There was no way to see in the warehouse, so they took a cab back to the *Walk in the Park*. Molly met them and they had a light lunch on board. The ship was remarkably well equipped for sabotage. Shorty wet suits, scuba gear, knives, radios, binoculars, a handgun, and duct tape. They relaxed on board until dark.

CHAPTER 42

▼

Luke drove a moped to a small dirt road on a hill 200 feet above the warehouse. He settled in with his radio, binoculars, bottled water, and a ham sandwich. He watched the sunset while listening to Tim McGraw on his iPod. Occasionally he took a quick look with the binoculars to check for action in front of the warehouse.

"Hey, Mol, where y'at," Luke said over the radio—familiar now that they had spent the afternoon killing time on the boat.

"I'm cool. Just watching the sun like you. Nice view from the top of your little boat."

Luke laughed. "Once I see them come out the building, you get your boys in the water. It won't take 'em long to get there."

Wade and Pete sat out of view near the transom—Wade calm as usual, Pete starting to get uptight.

"Relax. Quit tappin' ya foot," Wade said. "We can take one guy. If it's two, we don't do it. He won't know what hit him."

"I like this better than breaking into Carver's office. They're not going to call the cops on us," Pete said, as he fiddled with the zipper of his wetsuit.

"Yeah, that's a plus."

"You gonna stop in again to see the English chick with the bad teeth?"

"What makes you think I'm gonna do that?"

"Hey, don't get touchy. You can do what you want. I just figured since you mentioned her eyes and her accent and her tits. I think you mentioned her tits twice."

"You right, I thought about her a few times. She is a looker, especially if she keeps her mouth shut. So what's the deal with your pal, Buddy?"

"I haven't talked to him much. He says he knew nothing about Betts and his lab. I'm not sure I believe him." Still bitter, it gave him heartburn to think about it. "He has every reason to lie to me. I think he screwed me over. He's going to save his own hide before he's straight with me."

Over the radio. "OK, boys, in the drink."

Luke idled down the hill and kept an eye on the warehouse. Derek and another short black guy loaded the last of the boxes in a van and drove toward the harbor. Luke saw them drive by as he came up to the road. Not sure if they saw him, he turned the opposite way and made a U-turn after they were out of sight.

"Comin' your way, baby," Luke said to Molly. "White van, no markings 'cept a big crack in the front window."

"Boys are in. You tell me where they pull the van in." Molly got up on her knees for a better view but couldn't tell much with the lights' coming at her.

"There they are, dawlin'. Five slips up from you." Luke beeped as he passed.

"Five slips west of us boys. I can see one of those inflatable boats with an outboard. Two guys. One's Derek. The other guy's about the same size. They're moving the boxes now."

A 40-foot sailboat, moored in the middle of the harbor, was the only one with lights on. The boys ducked in and out of boats and positioned themselves half way between the loading spot and the sailboat. Loaded with boxes, the dude that wasn't Derek putted across the harbor. Pete and Wade adjusted their position in the water as he approached. When he got about half way to Pete and Wade, the driver turned around. The boys looked at each other and wondered if he made them. The driver pulled up to Derek again and had a brief conversation. He pointed out to the harbor and headed back out. Derek pulled away in the van.

The boys slipped under water until they could hear the engine get close. Pete knew not to breathe too fast but he couldn't help it. Sweat pooled in his mask and he fidgeted under the water. Wade made a quick flash of a light at Pete and they both sprung up onto the sides of the boat. The driver had that deer-in-the-headlights look—probably shit himself. Before he could blink, Wade had him in the water, knife to his neck. Pete killed the engine and pulled duct tape out of his wet suit.

"Not a damn word or I make shark bait." A quick nod—probably pissing now. "Who's on the boat?" No answer. Wade put the right amount of pressure with the blade. "Last time. Who's on the goddamn boat?"

"Dr. Wilhelm."

"Don't you mean Betts?" Pete said, tearing a piece of tape.

"No, he say Wilhelm."

"Big fat dude?"

"Yes, ugly like ox."

They taped his mouth and hands, and pushed his skinny butt back onto the boat. Then they made a mummy out of him with duct tape. Finally, they taped him to the boat. Back in the water, they made a wide sweep around the sailboat and approached from the back side. Wade went first. Betts was below deck. Wade removed his scuba gear and pulled a plastic bag out from his suit and removed the gun.

"Is that you, Rollie?" No answer. Pete recognized the voice. Betts stepped up from the cabin. He and Wade stood pointing their guns at each other.

"Who are you?" Betts asked, acting perplexed.

"We helpin' Rollie with his delivery. I know I don't want to fire this and you don't want any attention called to yourself—right?"

"Yes."

"Why don't we both put down these guns?"

Pete stepped up next to Wade. More deer-in-the-headlights look when Betts recognized Pete.

"Who's with you, doctor?" Wade asked.

"Alone I am."

"Good. Step back in the cabin. Sit, hands on your lap."

Pete followed behind Wade as Betts sat nervously in the cabin. Betts sat in shame as he faced the man whose wife he tossed overboard. Betts hung his head and his tangled hair fell across his forehead. He never wanted anyone to get hurt. Being tied to four murders and a kidnapping was not part of his plan. He never meant to injure Molly. He tossed her overboard only as a diversion. What bothered him most was the damage he caused to Buddy Duke's reputation. He began to consider suicide. He could see no way out of the mess. He reached to pick up his gun.

Pete sat across from him and unzipped his wetsuit. "Don't do it. You're going to answer some questions first." Betts looked up with resignation and placed the gun in front of him.

"What did Buddy know?"

"Nothing of this Buddy knows," tearing up.

"Why should I believe you?" relieved but skeptical.

"Buddy is my dear friend. Nothing I would do to make that bad. Buddy is no saint, but he has nothing to do with my shame."

"Then who is pulling the strings up in Washington?"

"Dick Coswell had Carver, Bennett, and Morgan thinking he was carrying out Buddy's orders. This, I did not know until the end."

"What about your oncology practice? You're just a sham. A fraud. Like Oz behind the curtain."

"Yes. You are right."

"How do you explain saving Buddy Duke's daughter?"

"This was, how you say, stupid luck."

"Dumb luck." Pete rolled his eyes.

"Yes. Some cancers remit all by themselves. I was in right place at right time."

"You are going to give yourself up tonight—confess to everything here and on Hilton Head. Yes?" Pete lifted the gun off the table.

"Yes."

Pete sat for a moment while conflicting emotions fought in his head. He knew this would be his last chance to give Betts a tongue lashing or a real lashing. The longer he sat, the more at peace he felt.

"Go take responsibility for what you did and clear Buddy's name. That's the least you can do. You're a pitiful little man."

"Gimme your cell phone," Wade barked at Betts. He pulled a card out of another plastic bag and dialed the number. "Margaret?…Hey, baby, it's Wade…Yeah, I'm gonna come see you…Listen, you know the chief of police?…Good. Call him and tell him to call me on this phone…Too long a story, cheré…I'll tell you the whole thing at dinner tomorrow.

Pete just smiled.

Wade held his arms out. "What?"

EPILOGUE

▼

Pete relaxed on a sofa in the cabin of the *Walk in the Park* as he talked to Buddy on the phone. Molly read a magazine with her legs stretched across his lap.

"I'm glad to hear it and I think you're making a good decision. I'll see you soon. Good bye, Buddy."

"What's new with the senator?" Molly peered over her magazine.

"Dick Coswell was arrested yesterday. Buddy gave up his run for president. He's going to come see us when we get back home."

"That's good to hear," Molly said.

"He says he's learned a lot from what happened."

"Good for him. How about you?" Molly put down her magazine. Pete thought for a minute.

"You know, Walt has made me think about some things. He's pretty sly. He gets you to understand things without actually telling you the answer."

Molly sat up and crossed her legs. "Maybe, that's because the answer isn't the same for everyone.

"I guess so," Pete said, turning to face Molly.

"So, what's *your* answer?"

"This took me a while to figure out. I think for me to have peace inside my head, I need to practice forgiveness. I need to stop being mad about things that happen to me and mad at other people. Mostly, I need to stop being mad at myself."

"Can you do that?"

"Yes. I thought I'd want to strangle Betts when we got to him. It felt good to control my feelings. I forgive him for his weaknesses. I forgive Billy Flick and I forgive myself for sitting there and letting him kill himself. And most of all, I forgive myself for almost getting you killed. I hope you'll forgive me."

"I never blamed you," Molly said as she leaned to Pete and embraced him.

"I love you, Molly Fredericks."

Luke and Wade appeared with four cold beers and a selection of hors d'oeuvres.

"Break it up, you two. It's time for a li'l celebration," Wade said.

"Stop waiting on us," Molly said to Luke.

"Owner's orders. I treat you like you own the boat until you testify and get your passports back."

"So how long this gonna take to convene a grand jury." Wade reached for a handful of nuts.

"Relax, mon. We on island time." Luke opened his beer.

Wade and Pete just smiled at each other.

0-595-67160-8

Printed in the United States
66121LVS00004B/38